Pages from
Patmos

Pages from Patmos

A New Testament Journey

Norman O'Banyon

PAGES FROM PATMOS
A NEW TESTAMENT JOURNEY

iUniverse books may be ordered through booksellers or by contacting:

iUniverse
1663 Liberty Drive
Bloomington, IN 47403
www.iuniverse.com
1-800-Authors (1-800-288-4677)

ISBN: 978-1-5320-0458-2 (sc)
ISBN: 978-1-5320-0459-9 (e)

Print information available on the last page.

iUniverse rev. date: 08/05/2016

Reader Notes: Name changes may be confusing. The practical identification of Apostles with common names required clarification. Transitioning from Hebrew to Greek helps the reader refocus to an expanding geographic audience:

Jesus called Simon, Peter;
Saul of Tarsus became Paul, a more Greek name;
Silvanus became known by his Hebrew name, Silas'
John, son of Silvanus, became John Mark, and then finally, Mark.
Joseph, a relative of John Mark, became known fondly as the "son of encouragement," Barnabas.

The Confirmation Class

Jerry liked this part of the old church. The classroom smelled like his Grandma's house, old, musty, and happy. His dad had told him that these classes were very important for him to receive information that would help him understand the church and the faith that was so important to all of his family. His older sister and brother had advised him that the sessions would be boring, but they always had cookies and cocoa at the end. Reverend Thomas Randle was the teacher who tried to make the classes at least a little interesting. He was also the junior high football coach, so Jerry made at least some effort to listen.

Pastor Randle said, "The drawing you have in front of you is a way for us to learn about the Bible. Bonnie, my wife, made it so you can understand that the word 'Bible' means 'books'. She drew two bookcases for us. The one on the left represents the Old Testament, the Jewish Scriptures. There are forty-six books on the five shelves. The top shelf… do you see it?… are the books of Moses, called the Law. They are Genesis, Exodus, Leviticus, Numbers, and Deuteronomy. The second shelf of our library is called the Prophets, which are mostly very old history and sermons. Since the first books were actually scrolls of rough paper made from papyrus, they were limited in length, so Samuel had to use two scrolls to get it all written: First and Second Samuel. Why do you suppose there is also a First and Second Kings?"

Shelly, the smartest girl in the class answered, "Because there were so many kings?"

"Exactly!" Mr. Randle said with a grin. "There are twenty-one books on that shelf which is called the Major Prophets. It's not because they were more important than the next shelf, but longer. The next shelf is called the Minor Prophets, not because of their age, but they are shorter. There are twelve books on that shelf.

A Very Long While Ago

The oil lamps cast silhouettes on the walls and a gentle warm glow on the faces of those seated comfortably around the table. All the preparations were complete as the guests arrived. The house had been thoroughly cleaned and all leavening removed. Because Silvanus, the host, was once again away on Roman assignment in the region of Cilicia, his brother-in-law, Joseph from Cyprus, was given the task of hosting the feast. Silvanus' wife, Mary, John's mother, began the singing when she could see two stars in the evening sky. Passover Sabbath was beginning. There were ten, as the Jewish law required, seated; most of them were also from the island of Cyprus, but now living in Jerusalem. A prayer was spoken and Joseph nodded to ten-year-old John, his nephew, who played an important role as the youngest present. In his clear soprano voice the lad asked, "Why is this night different from all other nights?"

Joseph rose and retold the story of the ancestor's captivity in Egypt stemming from the famine in Israel. On the table was a roasted leg of lamb signifying the paschal Lamb; unleavened bread, representing the haste with which they departed captivity; a roasted egg represented the sacrifice; bitter herbs represented the hardship of slavery; salt water was a reminder of four hundred years of tears; a mixture of apples, nuts, and wine, called *haroset* symbolized the mortar from which they made bricks for Pharaoh's projects; and finally, a green vegetable represented new life. It was a meal with an honored story. Gladly, Joseph told of the exodus of their people, interspersed by the four promises of God from the Exodus scroll, represented by cups of wine mixed with water. "I will free you," Joseph's voice was strong and clear. They all took a small drink. "I will deliver you." They took another sip of wine. "I will redeem you." He emphasized the word "redeem". Once again they took a sip. Finally, he quoted, "I will take you as my people." They drank again, grateful for their heritage and this memorable setting.

"The Passover feast is drawing to a close now," Joseph's voice was hushed dramatically. "With the pouring of one more cup for the prophet Elijah, who is expected to return during the Passover to announce the day of the Lord, we wait eager for God to usher in the time of Messiah." With the final blessing, the children were invited to leave the table and search through the house to find the hidden matsah treat. Once discovered, it would be shared by them as the last item to be eaten at the meal. John had some insider knowledge of the hiding places, so just for fun he tried to make the search last a little extra long to make the reward taste a little extra sweet.

The civil service life of Silvanus, who had missed his family's Passover meal, had begun in his father's lending bank. His extensive training in Greek law and language skills made him an enormous asset to the bank. By devoted service to customers and limited risk-taking, the bank had flourished and developed a trustworthy reputation. The Governor's legate had approached Silvanus to be an occasional arbitrator between the Jews and Greeks, using both his knowledge of law and just negotiation skills. There were a number of successful interventions, and Silvanus was asked to become a tax arbiter. That post was done in such a competent manner; he was given the responsibility of the northern districts of Pontius Pilate's authority. His task was to visit each principality, accompanied by a century of Roman soldiers, collecting the Roman tribute. One quarter of the tax was delivered to the treasury of Governor Pilate, and the larger share was sent to Rome for the Emperor's treasury. The legate instructed Silvanus to add a one percent surcharge to the tribute as his compensation. It became a task that kept him away from home for at least the first four months of the year, while building a large surplus balance in his bank account.

In his eighth year as Tribute Consul, Silvanus was asked by the legate about a proposal Governor Pilate had for creating greater security in the northern provinces. He had conceived of a plan for a prison to be constructed in Antioch of Syria. By adding another one percent surcharge to the tribute, he could have a place of detention or execution. It would be a physical expression of Pilate's authority.

A Sinister Plan

By his return to Jerusalem the following spring, Silvanus had a concept that he thought might appeal to the legate.

"The concept is sound, sir, to show the breadth and strength of the Governor's reach," he began. "However, more prisons are not needed to maintain the obedience of the population by confinement, but by the perception of power, the idea of control. If the prison is built in Antioch, it will require a large building site and extensive expenditures for secure walls and cells. However, if the Governor would grant me the use of one of the small, barren, uninhabited islands off the coast, I could create the concept of a terrible place of abandonment and starvation. We could name it, 'Plecto Claustrum,' or 'Death Dungeon.' Just the thought of exile there would build the Governor's reputation. Just the fear of it would match the offensive force of a century of soldiers."

"Are you suggesting, Silvanus, that you would undertake the cost of this project yourself?"

"The greatest cost would be the Governor's grant of using an empty island as a new prison. I will only add to the image of it. I can circulate stories of starvation and madness from isolation." His smile at such an outlandish notion was contagious.

The legate chuckled, knowing that Silvanus had found a way to oblige the Governor's need for greater respect without tapping into the tribute coffers. "I'll make the suggestion to him myself. You may have found a way to save us significant expense and yet accomplish our intent." He was thinking how he would get the credit for this idea, and Silvanus would get the task of it.

"Remember," he said to Silvanus adding a dimension never promised, "You pledged your own funds to make this a reality. We will want routine updates on its development."

Within a fortnight Silvanus had a sealed proclamation that Patmos Island would henceforth be known as the location of Death Dungeon, the Governor's new prison.

Good News

Two other milestones happened that summer. John completed his studies to become a Son of the Law; his bar mitzvah was celebrated by a large gathering of family and friends from Cyprus. Secondly, Joseph introduced Silvanus to the teachings of a carpenter from Nazareth. "He doesn't claim to be a rabbi or a prophet, but I see him as both. He begins with old promises made to our fore-fathers and shows us how they lead us to a deeper, truer, more hopeful understanding of God's covenant with Israel. I've only heard him speak twice, but both times my heart was touched. Jesus says that the Kingdom of God is near to us."

Joseph shook his head in disbelief.

"He teaches not just the men who come to hear him, but women, outcasts, sinners. It doesn't seem to make a difference with him what you are. He says that God's pure and holy love is for each and every one of us."

Joseph was still for a moment, remembering a special teaching. "He told a story to demonstrate who our neighbor should be, about a traveler who was set upon by robbers who nearly killed him. A priest and a Levite came to where the man was lying in the dirt. They offered no assistance, but a cursed Samaritan cared for him and carried him to a shelter where he could receive comfort. Can you believe a story that has a Samaritan as a hero? It was nearly as shocking to us as it was to the understanding of the pious listeners when they heard of a priest and a Levite offering no mercy at all." Joseph shook his head again, then finished, "But when I heard it my heart thrilled at the story. God's love is for all of us."

Silvanus made a mental note that on his way north in just a couple months, he would pass through Capernaum, where this teacher seemed to be located. If nothing else it would show his brother-in-law that he respected his suggestion. He also reminded himself of the importance of speaking to John about his education path. Now that he was a Son of the Law, it was time to think about his future occupation. Vespius, the Light of Literature and Journal Accounting for the Greek community, agreed to add him as a new student. As long as there would be taxes to pay, there would be a need for arbitration. It had been a satisfying and lucrative career for Silvanus. If John preferred to relate to the Hebrew community, there were two tent makers that had agreed to teach him the craft. The drawback from that career was the spiritual implications of dealing with unclean dead animal skins. It was time for the lad to make some choices. As it turned out John would spend four years in the tutelage of Vespius, learning to craft accurate accounts of the business of politicians or decrees of government. He was an apt student with an eager mind.

A New Believer

The following summer when he had completed his northern duties, Silvanus was sharing an excited conversation with Joseph. "You were correct. He is a most unusual teacher. Usually the rabbi quotes some other famous rabbinic saying and then tries to explain it in detail. The one they call Jesus simply opens his heart to the people in a very winsome manner. I saw a leper come up to him and kneel down saying, 'Lord, if you will, you can make me clean.' Think of that! We could see how infected he was, but the teacher stretched out his hand and touched him. Instead of becoming infected himself, he just said, 'I will; be clean.' And immediately his leprosy was cleansed. The teacher said to him, 'See that you say nothing to anyone; but go, show yourself to the priest, and offer the gift that Moses commanded, for a proof to the people.' It was the most gracious thing I have ever seen."

Joseph replied softly, "But many of us know that he is far more than a teacher. We believe he is the promised One of God."

Silvanus nodded with a smile. "Yes, my heart was moved as well. One day I joined a group of people who had gathered around him near the water's edge. Fishermen were cleaning their nets after a weary night of fishing. Jesus advised them to put back out into the lake. The big one called Simon, said, 'We tried in vain all night, but at your word, we will try a bit more.' When they let down their net, it was so filled with fish it was about to burst. Simon shouted for two other fishermen on the shore to come and help pull in the enormous catch. When they were back on dry land, Simon told Jesus that he was an unworthy man to be in the presence of the teacher, but Jesus told them to follow him as disciples and they would be fishers of men. It was a scene I will never forget."

Joseph nodded again and said, "Wherever he goes signs and wonders follow. Healings happen; insight to old lessons is learned; the hopeless find courage and the lost are found. I am eager to be with him again soon."

"I'm feeling the same way, brother. I have a reason to look forward to my northern journeys now. Do you think he will come to Jerusalem at all?"

"Perhaps, but I'm also sure he knows how politically charged this city is. He may want the serenity of the countryside to forge his lessons." Joseph was quiet for a moment before adding, "I wonder if he can heal our willingness to wage war on one another."

Silvanus had a momentary thought of the three families arrested for failure to pay their taxes. The law required to have them arrested and sold as slaves, or more severe punishment. He had them moved to Didyma and placed on a freighter carrying construction material, fruit trees and grape starts. Their slave-labor punishment would be to help build their new homes on a deserted island. He answered Joseph, "The name I heard the people call him is, 'Prince of Peace.' It would truly be a new age of compassion if he could accomplish that miracle."

A Report of Success

When Silvanus made his report to the legate, indicating that once again there had been an increased tribute from each region, he reported that five properties had been confiscated and sold for unpaid tribute. In addition, three families were sent to Plecto Claustrum as slave labor under the security of three guards. They were to begin excavating the dungeon and erecting the guards' quarters. It was a report that brought him positive recognition and personal satisfaction.

The following year there was an even more positive report for the legate. The principalities all paid promptly. Seven properties were confiscated for unpaid tribute, and four families more were sent to the "Dungeon" as slave laborers. The confiscations were profitable to all except the previous owners. Using his own funds, Silvanus paid the debt to the tribute, usually for less than a tenth its value. He then frequently rented the property to a neighbor who was happy to increase the size of his holding. Silvanus not only profited by these rentals, he increased the threat of nonpayment. Wherever he travelled the announcement of the Governor's new dungeon became an ominous threat. It was an even greater danger than the century of Roman guards that accompanied him.

Joseph was again reporting on the activity of the Nazarene. "He sent seventy two of us to go as teams ahead of him to determine the openness of the villages. Where we were welcomed, amazing things happened. It was as if we were accompanied by angels. The sick and lame were strengthened and healed. People who had lost their hope were revitalized. Some who were carrying grudges found forgiveness; some who were alienated were reunited. If they were hostile or suspicious of us, we simply knocked the dust of their road off our sandals and like prophets from the past, we left that place. I've never felt more useful, or invigorated. And the listeners, whether they are ardent or simply curious, the numbers are growing all the time.

"One day he went far into the wilderness to pray," Joseph said softly. "A very large crowd followed him, hoping for more teaching or healing. When it was time to eat, his followers wondered where all these people could find food." His eyes sparkled as he continued, "Jesus asked the disciples what they had to share. They could only come up with five little loaves and two fish. Jesus told them to bring the food to him. He had the people sit down. He blessed the loaves and fishes and began distributing it amongst the people. This is amazing," Joseph said almost with glee. "When everyone had eaten the disciples gathered the left-over food. It filled twelve baskets!" Joseph had a wonderful smile as he added, "Jesus said that he came to bring us life in abundance. That day the abundance was very visible. I'll never forget it."

Another Passover

It was time for Passover again. Preparations were underway for an unusual feast. Silvanus was once again in the northern districts, but this year Joseph was travelling with Jesus and his disciples. Mary was carefully explaining why John would have the responsibility of being the host. "Your aunt will be here with three other families from Cyprus. Your cousin Benjamin is nine years old and can ask the question, if you will carefully instruct him."

John shrugged modestly. "I have heard Uncle Joseph tell the story so many times, I know it by heart. I will try to do a faithful account of the meaning of our feast."

As Mary looked at her son, she wondered if he had grown wiser as well as taller for a fifteen-year-old.

"The Teacher, Vespius, says I have a keen sense of keeping the facts clear in the accounts I record. I will try not to embarrass you or Uncle Joseph."

The table was filled with eager faces as Mary sang a familiar song and spoke the Passover prayer. With only a bit of coaxing, young Benjamin asked the proper question, "Why is this night different from all other nights?"

Then John said in a clear voice, "You have heard the reading. 'And the angel of the Lord appeared to Moses in a flame of fire out of the midst of a bush; and he looked and lo, the bush was burning, yet it was not consumed....Then the Lord said, 'I have seen the affliction of my people, who are in Egypt, and have heard their cry because of their taskmaster; I know their sufferings, and I have come down to deliver them out of the hand of the Egyptians, and to bring them up out of that land to a good and broad land, a land flowing with milk and honey...'"

John looked from face to face, some familiar, others new. Then he said, "Tonight we do not have a burning bush, but oil lamps to light our table. We do not have an angel of the Lord speaking mysteriously to us, but we do have this feast that reminds us of a Great God who still delivers us out of tribulation and provides for our needs."

Then carefully he identified the various ingredients of the feast and their significance. He retold the familiar account of deliverance as he had heard it. John remembered to toast the promises of God with cups of wine mixed with water and to pour a cup for Elijah who was to return. With the final blessing, Mary began another hymn that all could sing. It had been a wonderful Passover feast.

When the guests were gone and John was alone with his mother, he asked a question that had been on his mind for a long time. "Mother I mean no disrespect for father. Can you explain why the Passover is so important to us, but he has never attended? Is he at another table partaking of the feast?"

Mary answered with a sad smile, "Son, I assumed you understood. Your father is in the service of the Roman Prefect. It is his privilege to gather the tribute taxes collected by the Northern provinces. He goes as a buffer between the harsh demands of the Romans and those who have been bled to the extent of their ability. His duty keeps him far away from us, but his heart is always with us first of all. When he was a boy he was from a Greek home and was carefully taught their beliefs. They looked to other gods than Jehovah."

"But there is no other god than the Lord God," the confused lad said.

"That is the foundation of our faith. Greeks believe in gods that take on the likeness of men, while our God has created us in his own image and looks to us for obedience. Your father became a Jew when he came here for schooling. He came to rejoice in the God of Abraham and all that he gave us as a people. Your father loves the Law, and he loves us deeply. He has found a way to provide us with this wonderful home and the security of keeping our faith. I have always felt that the only thing that would bless him more is the opportunity to share the festival feasts with us."

"Is that why he keeps the Greek form of his Name? If he claimed his Jewish identity," John wondered aloud, "would he lose his station as a Tax Consul for the Governor?"

"Yes, I suppose he would," his mother answered thoughtfully. "I can scarcely imagine that a Roman would allow a Jew to be so closely involved with his treasury."

"Then I must pray for father's safety while he is travelling, and for God's guidance in choosing my future for I will not be able to follow in father's footsteps. I have dreamt of a day when I would have something to say and people would listen. Father has such authority he only needs to whisper and the entire province listens."

"Do you have any thoughts what your career might be?" His mother's warm eyes were compelling.

"The Teacher, Vespius, says that I have an aptitude for records and bookkeeping. Perhaps there is someone of importance who will need my services one day." John shrugged in curiosity. "I've never been far from the walls of Jerusalem. I would love to be able to see more of our world."

For a moment his mother thought of the many dangers beyond their secure walls. A second thought wondered just how secure those walls might be with growing discontent in the Jewish community, opposing the mighty power of Rome.

Another Report of Growth

The return of Silvanus was a time of celebration. Once again he had surpassed the previous collection of tribute. Once again there had been a confiscation of properties and the imprisonment of six families in the "Dungeon." When the legate received his report, there was a wide smile of satisfaction. Silvanus reported that all through the region of northern Syria and Cilicia the Governor's authority carried the threat of terrible imprisonment. The bodies of those unable to survive the horrible conditions were simply cast from the cliff of the remote island into the sea. The threat was complete and ominous.

Joseph was eager to hear a different report; one of the encounters Silvanus had with the teacher whom many were now calling "The Promised One."

"His miracles were frequently accompanied by the command to tell no one about the marvelous moment. Can you imagine," Silvanus asked, "the father of the revived daughter, who all thought was dead, telling no one that Jesus had simply taken her cold hand saying, 'Little girl I say to thee, arise'? It's unthinkable! The joy of that father spilled out to many when his little girl was fully recovered and dancing in their midst. Peter and John were there and saw it themselves." Silvanus was uncharacteristically emotional. "We must tell of these miraculous moments."

"As I was passing through Galilee," he continued, "I heard an account of a man so possessed by demons that he had to be chained near the tombs. He was so filled with destruction that he tore the chains apart and injured his own body. Yet when Jesus approached him and simply asked him, 'What is your name?' the man became calm and rational. The man told Jesus that his name was 'Legion' for he was so confused. Jesus commanded the demons to come out of the man, who was healed immediately. The man wanted to join Jesus' followers, but was told to go back to Decapolis and tell others about his experience."

The two spent most of the evening retelling amazing stories of Jesus' wonders.

When it was nearly time to put out the oil lamps, Silvanus said, "I heard of an encounter Jesus had with a rich young man who was seeking eternal life. Jesus said to him, 'If you would enter life, keep the commandments.' When the young man acknowledged that he had done that, he asked 'What do I still lack?' Then Jesus said to him, 'If you would be perfect, go, sell what you possess and give it to the poor, and you will have treasures in heaven; and come, follow me.'" Silvanus shook his head. "Sadly the young man went away because he had great possessions. When I heard that, I wondered if I would ever be so moved to fulfill that request. I'm concerned that his demands are beyond reason."

Joseph was still for a bit before he answered, "I'm concerned that one who has such a strong following is talking about his own death and resurrection." Both men were still, looking into the shadows of their own thoughts.

A Challenging Assignment

Vespius admired John's focus and reliability; after three years, it was time for him to demonstrate his skill in recording the essence of the past.

"John you have completed our introduction with skill and understanding. You Jews claim great guidance from the Law and the Prophets. We can read the Law and argue its meaning. I would like you to write an account clarifying the Prophets and their significance to the Hebrews. You have two weeks to complete the assignment. Is that clear? Do you have any questions?"

"Would you like the composition to be written in Greek or Hebrew?"

"You may be reminding me," the Teacher said with a wry smile, "that few students have your skill in more languages than Greek. Since it will have a wider audience if it is written in Greek, I suggest you use Greek, the one that may be a bit less comfortable for you."

John had instant enthusiasm for the assignment, and determined that conversations with his uncle Joseph would not be beyond the allowable range of research.

John wrote:

> A prophet is not a seer who peers into the crystal-clear stream water of the future and sees more than the stones of a streambed. Prophet means spokesman; the one who with unfathomable audacity claims to speak for the Lord God, the Creator of heaven and earth. There is no evidence that a prophet ever had political power or even many friends.

One day some city boys followed along behind the prophet Elisha, calling him 'Bald-head!' Elisha called a curse down on the boys, which immediately brought two bears upon them. That day forty two were mauled by the bears and the prophet continued on his way to Mount Carmel. (Second scroll of Kings) Popularity was never a consideration with the prophets, nor political acclaim.

The prophet Jeremiah shows a clay pot to a crowd of Judeans and told them that it represented Judah. Then he smashes it to shards and told them that this was an example of how God would repair their faithlessness. (The scroll of Jeremiah) He was unpopular, but quite correct in his prediction.

In a dream the prophet Ezekiel eats a copy of the Law from start to finish to show how sweet as honey was the word of God. (The scroll of Ezekiel)

In the time of the prophet Amos, the Israelites looked forward to the day when the Lord God would finally come and deliver them from their afflictions. Amos told them they would be wise to look forward to something else because when the day came, the Lord would be fierce with the unbelievers, but would deal with Israel's disobedience first. Quoting God, Amos went on to say, "I hate and despise your religious feasts; I can't stand your assemblies." He went on, "Away with the noise of your songs! I will not listen to the music of your harps. But let justice roll on like a river, righteousness like a never-failing stream!" (The scroll of Amos)

Jeremiah was thrown into a cistern, and the rumor is that Isaiah was sawed in half. We are left to guess how Amos was mistreated.

When the unknown prophet who penned the final section of the Isaiah scroll pondered the question, "What were the Chosen People chosen for?" his answer was that they were chosen not to overwhelm the world in triumph but to suffer and die for the world in love. Describing the prophet, these harsh words are used, "He was despised and rejected by men, a man of sorrows and familiar with suffering. Like one from whom men will hide their faces, he was despised, and we esteemed him not."

The prophets were drunk on God, and in their intoxicated presence no one was ever comfortable. With the total lack of tact they roared out against deception and corruption wherever they found them. Prophets were the terror of kings and priests. The prophet Nathan tells King David to his face that he is an adulterer and murderer. (The second scroll of Samuel) The prophet Jeremiah went straight to the Temple itself and said,

"Do not trust these deceptive words! This is the Temple of the Lord, the Temple of the Lord, the Temple of the Lord." (The scroll of Jeremiah)

It was like a prophet to say it three times to make it a fact.

The point might be made that the prophets all had moments of madness. Hosea marries Gomer the prostitute to dramatize Israel's inability to practice fidelity. Elijah got into a fire contest with the prophets of Baal, then after winning, he had to flee and hide on Mount Horeb. Ezekiel had a vision of a wheel with spokes and a rim with something like eyes. The unusual object could be still on the ground or fly in the air making frightening sounds. A voice thundered from above that Israel's choice was either to return to its faithful obedience or suffer a dire consequence. He also had the vision of speaking to a valley covered with dead and dry bones. A voice told him to prophesy to the bones, which when he speaks, reconnect with one another at the sound of his voice, but they were still lifeless. Once again he prophesied to the bones and the breath, or wind, or spirit of God filled them, and a mighty army stood strong.

It could be summed up that all the prophets who quarreled with a disobedient Israel were deep in a lover's quarrel. If they didn't have a burning love for Israel they probably would never have bothered to tell it that it was headed for destruction. They would have simply let it go. But their quarrel was Jehovah's quarrel, and at stake was the Covenant promise. It was a quarrel well worth the high cost.

Before the short scroll was delivered to the Teacher, John asked his uncle to preview it for accuracy. With his compliments, the work was handed to Vespius. A few days later they chatted about his assignment.

"In the main," The Teacher began, "your work captured the task well. You kept my interest while giving a fair, if not exhaustive view of the prophets. It could have been more comprehensive; there were many unmentioned prophets. Over all this is an excellent work for a beginning student. It is apparent the Greek is not well polished, and at times feels immature. There was a tendency for you to drift into the present history with your verb confusions. For example, Jeremiah *shows a clay pot to a crowd*. Then he *smashes it to shards*. In a dream the prophet Ezekiel *eats a copy of the Law, Nathan tells King David* to his face, *Hosea marries Gomer* the prostitute are some of the ways in which you speak of events from the past in a present tense verb. It is immature, yet quite enthralling to the reader, placing him at the scene, so to speak. Above all, your conclusion was most effective, suggesting that the prophets were in fact a lover's quarrel between Jehovah and Israel. It was a completely successful writing. Well done! We still have much work to do, however."

Jesus Is Near

One chilly winter evening, a friend came to the house to give Joseph news that was both expected and worrisome. Jesus and his followers were coming south. They had already passed through Jericho.

The man said earnestly, "We could hardly believe that the tax collector named Zachaeus had climbed a tree so he could have a clear view of Jesus. The entire town was talking how he responded when Jesus stopped under the tree and told him to climb down and host a dinner. The tax collector actually said he would give half of his wealth to the poor and he would pay back anyone he had defrauded fourfold. Jesus told him that salvation had come to his house. Isn't that an amazing story?"

The visitor had one more account to report. "Then, as Jesus was leaving Jericho, an old blind man named Bartimaeus heard the noise of their passing, and shouted out, 'Jesus, Son of David, have mercy on me!' They tried to quiet him because he was making a Messianic claim, but Jesus stopped and said, 'Call him.' Immediately the blind man jumped to his feet, and told the Master that he just wanted to see. Jesus replied to him, 'Go, your faith has healed you.' Granted, I was not there, but those who were swear that the old man received his sight immediately and followed after the crowd. I think Jesus is going to spend some time in Bethany, and then he will be in Jerusalem for Passover. They need to find some lodging. Do you think you could help with that? I know the city is very full at this time."

"My sister often offers the roof terrace of this house to pilgrims. I'll see if she has promised it to anyone else."

So it was that those whom Joseph had travelled far to follow were to spend several days in this very house. Oh, the unusual pathway of fate.

With Silvanus once again caring for his tribute duties in the north, Joseph had only John to tell the latest accounts of the wonders of Jesus.

"There was the storm on the Sea of Galilee," an excited Joseph said. "The followers were certain their boat was about to be overwhelmed by the wind and the waves. Jesus simply commanded, 'Peace be still,' and the storm was gone. Can you imagine?"

John, who had not been part of the earlier stories, admitted that in fact, he couldn't imagine someone giving instructions to the elements.

Undaunted, Joseph continued, "There is a report that Jesus received news that his close friend Lazarus, who lived in Bethany, was quite ill. When Jesus finally arrived there, the man's sisters, Mary and Martha, were in grief because four days prior they had laid their brother's deceased body in the tomb. They scolded Jesus for waiting so long. Jesus simply asked them, 'Did I not tell you that if you believed, you would see the glory of God?' They removed the tomb stone and Jesus prayed, then he called Lazarus out of the tomb."

"No, he could not," John murmured, "not after four days."

"Oh, yes," Joseph said in a hushed voice. "Lazarus stepped out of the tomb, and Jesus commanded them to take the grave clothes off of him and let him go."

"Does he only do miracles?" the now curious lad asked.

"Far from it. On the mountainside he spoke to a large crowd, explaining God's blessings, and he has very many stories about how we can more fully live in peace with our neighbor and with the Lord God. He makes us think about a deeper ethic. For example, he told a story about a man who had two sons, whom he asked to work in the vineyard. One said he would do it, but the other said he would not. The first one failed to keep his promise, and the other had a change of heart. Even though he had initially said 'no,' he completed the work. Now which one did the will of the father, the one who said 'yes' but didn't, or the one who said 'no' and did? It makes you think, doesn't it?"

Jesus In the Terrace

For nearly a month John listened to his uncle's accounts of Jesus. John wondered at the wisdom contained in such short, memorable sayings. Then six days before Passover, Joseph told him that Jesus was in Bethany. Joseph had been invited to a dinner with the followers,

"And tomorrow they will come into the Temple. Because we have pilgrims using the terrace for a few days, they will return to Bethany each night. It's only 15 stadia, a short hour's walk. On the first night of the Feast of Unleavened Bread, they will use the terrace while we share our meal down here." There was a trembling excitement in his announcement. If he had known the way the evening was about to end, he would have been trembling with dread.

When the night of the Seder Feast arrived, the house was once again cleaned of all leavening. Extra lamps were lit to chase away shadows because the table was filled beyond capacity. Several of the men from Cyprus, who had arrived with Jesus, were welcomed guests, while the upper terrace room was being used by Jesus and the close followers. A half of a lamb had been roasted; the front quarter for the upper room and the larger portion for the lower table. Uncle Joseph was once again the host, but he was having some difficulty bringing everyone's attention to the traditional feast. They wanted to talk about the amazing week they had just shared.

One man remembered the dinner at Bethany. "A sister brought in a jar of ointment and sprinkled it on Jesus' feet. The house was filled with the pleasant fragrance of it, but Judas protested that the expensive oil could have been sold to ease the plight of the poor. Jesus told him to leave her alone. The oil was intended for his burial. He reminded us all that the poor would always be with us, but he would not. It was a beautiful yet eerie moment."

Another man recalled how the people reacted when the cloaks were spread on the donkey, and Jesus rode down from the Mount of Olives. They gathered alongside the road, some waving branches and others putting their cloaks on the road. It was the sort of scene that made them think of a king coming to a city in peace. Many of them were singing Psalms or shouting 'Hosanna', which is Hebrew for 'save us.' It felt like a victory parade."

Yet another said, "I'd never been in Jerusalem, so when he entered the Temple I was awestruck. When he began overturning tables and chasing away those moneychangers, I was sure we would be arrested. He seemed calm, almost sad that he had to restore a level of reverence there."

A man near uncle Joseph said, "I will never forget yesterday, when in the Temple he told a story about a coming judgment. Only after thinking about the content of his teaching did I understand that there are several levels of meaning. He said that when the Son of Man comes in glory, accompanied by angels, he would separate the people as a shepherd separates the sheep from the goats. To those on his right hand he will welcome them into an inheritance, the kingdom prepared for them since the creation of the world. For he was hungry, and they had fed him; thirsty and they had given him something to drink. He had been a stranger, and they welcomed him; he needed clothes, and they gave him something to wear. He had been sick, and they cared for him, in prison, and they visited him. The righteous were surprised and asked the King, 'When did we do that for you?' And he answered, 'When you did it to one of the least of these brothers of mine, you did it for me.'"

"Then the King will say to those on his left, 'Depart from me you who are cursed, into the eternal fire prepared for the devil and his angels. For I was hungry and you gave me nothing to eat; I was thirsty and you gave me nothing to drink. I was a stranger and you did not welcome me in; I needed clothes and you gave me nothing to wear. I was sick and in prison and you did not look after me.' The condemned were surprised and asked, 'When did we not do that for you?' He replied, 'I tell you the truth, whatever you did not do for one of the least of these, you did not do for me.' Then they will go away to eternal punishment, but the righteous to eternal life."

Before another story could begin, Mary drew their attention back to the Seder by singing a song of gratitude. When they finished the song, young Benjamin asked that important question, "Why is this night different from all other nights?"

A Rude Interruption

Joseph loved the story of deliverance from Egypt and carefully wove the history of their people through the feast. Just as they were lifting the fourth cup, recalling God's promises, they were interrupted by the sound of heavy feet hurrying up the stairs to the terrace. There was a growl of angry voices, and then the footsteps came rattling back down. A heavy knock on the door was immediately followed by the door being roughly forced open. A squad of the High Priest's Temple guards burst into the room.

"We are here to arrest the Nazarene called Jesus!" one of them barked. Joseph recognized one of Jesus followers in the group and was suddenly alert to betrayal.

"As you can see," Joseph's voice was submissive, "we are Jews from Cyprus, here as guests of Silvanus of Salamis, Cyprus, Tribute Consul for Pontius Pilate."

The brutish group was roughly examining each man at the table.

"I know where they have gone," the follower of Jesus said finally. "Their plan is to go to the Garden of Gethsemane for prayer. You can find him there." Without another word he turned toward the door. The disorderly crowd carrying clubs and swords followed him into the darkness of the street without one word of apology for their rudeness.

The room was in shocked silence until John whispered, "I must warn him! If they go out the Essene Gate, I might have a quicker way if I hurry to the Water Gate by the pool of Siloam." He was only wearing his tunic, but the night was not cold and his task was urgent.

A Journey Fuelled By Fear

His route would have been quicker at any other time of year, but with the glut of pilgrims in Jerusalem for Passover, the streets were crowded. Twice he had to apologize for nearly knocking someone over. By the time he got through the gate and down the long steps, he was sure his task was futile. Still he hurried on, for the guards may have been detained by crowds as well.

Once in the olive grove, he began listening for raised voices or watching for groups of men. He thought there might be something happening a bit to his right. He was in such a hurry he failed to be cautious and stumbled nearly into the center of the chaos. The one who led the guards had approached Jesus and saying, "Hail, rabbi," he kissed him. It must have been a signal, for suddenly the guards were grabbing men, and clubs were flying. One of the Temple bullies managed to grab John by the knap of his neck. Fortunately no club or sword was used. If he had been wearing his outer robe and belt, he would surely have been captured. As it was he was able to twist around so his head was toward his captor. Then it was a matter of raising his arms and wiggling out of the tunic. He scrambled back into the shadows as quickly as he had arrived. Now his route was back up the Hinnom Valley, the way the guards had gotten there before him. Naked and embarrassed, John stayed in the shadows as much as he could, and wept tears of failure and fear all the way home. ★(Mark 14:51)

Unbelievable News

John entered the side door, which allowed him to reach his room unnoticed. With a fresh tunic, he joined the men who were still agitated around the table. One said, "It's bad enough to put up with the cruelty of the Romans, but these were our own people." Another agreed saying, "The Temple guards are to look after our safety, not threaten us with clubs and swords." The one standing next to Joseph said, "They showed no respect for the Seder."

John eased near his uncle and said softly, "They arrested Jesus. He was betrayed by one of his own followers."

Joseph looked into John's eyes and asked for clarity, "You are certain they captured him?"

The lad simply nodded. "I think they were after them all, but most escaped into the shadows, just as I did."

His uncle draped his hand over the young strong shoulder. "I praise you for your effort. The rest of us just stood here offended. You at least made a heroic attempt to intervene. I'm proud of you and know that your father will feel the same way."

They had no way of knowing the abuse Jesus was receiving at the hands of the Temple guards, the mockery and insults. The high priest had no authority to execute, so charges were fabricated. Jesus was taken to Governor Pilate, who tried his best to avoid their demands. Finally, however, with threats that would undermine his status in Rome, he agreed to execute Jesus along with two criminals. Jesus was flogged and forced to carry his own cross outside the city to the place of the skull. There they crucified him.

The Regrouping of Faith

Sometime during that long night Joseph heard a knock at the door. It didn't sound threatening, so cautiously he opened it to find most of the followers standing in the darkness. Shyly the one called Simon asked, "We have nowhere to go and need a place to hide, or weep, or pray. May we rest in the terrace room?"

"Of course, you are welcome here." He led them to the stairway and said, "There is a door up there that can be bolted for privacy. We'll bring you water and food in the morning." The frightened men graciously received his hospitality.

A deep pall held the house on the following day. It was made unbearable when the follower known as John, son of Zebedee, brought news that Jesus had been crucified and his body was being buried in a nearby tomb. The sound of weeping was constant for hours.

The next day was Sabbath. When John took a tray of bread and cheese to the upper room, the one called Simon greeted him. "You were in the garden, weren't you?" John nodded and the question continued. "You came to warn us. Do you live in this house?"

"Yes. Silvanus the Tribute Consul is my father and Mary is my mother. You know her as the sister of Joseph."

"We give thanks for your hospitality. This is a day when we all feel lost. It helps to think of your courage to come to warn us. I saw the guard grab you, but honestly we were all running for the safety of the darkness. How did you escape?" His warm eyes made John feel like a young comrade.

"He didn't grab me, but my tunic." His voice was soft with embarrassment. "Like a fox I wiggled free from it and ran home naked."

The men standing nearby smiled, in spite of the incredible sorrow of the morning. They could imagine the humor in the escape. One of them said, "You were a young Adam, running from the Garden."

Simon asked, "Will you tell us your name?"

"I'm John, son of Silvanus of Cyprus."

"Please convey to your father and mother our deep gratitude for this hospitality and your courageous effort last night. I believe your uncle was one of the seventy-two that went out ahead of Jesus. If he would like to join us in prayer, we would be blessed even more. Of course you are also welcome. We need all the courage we can find." The lightness of the previous moment was gone, carried away in the tide of grief common to them all.

Joseph spent most of the day in the terrace with the followers. John said he was going to return to the Gethsemane Garden to see if he could find his tunic. Actually he was not comfortable in the presence of these men whose lives were so directed by faith and the dedication to their spiritual guide. It was probably as well that he didn't find the tunic. He had already broken the Sabbath restriction of the distance he was permitted to walk. If he had found it he would have been tempted to pick it up, another violation, shake the dirt off of it, and carry it home, all violations of the Sabbath. John smiled, thinking that to him the tunic was worth those slight violations.

He arrived home just in time to carry a large tray of bread, boiled fish and figs for the guests on the terrace. An additional handful of men had joined them, grateful for the security and hospitality. When John placed the tray on the table, he could see how welcome it was. Joseph explained that it was not only the food that these men needed, but John's skill as a recording secretary. There had been some confusions during the afternoon as they recalled the wondrous days spent with Jesus. They were having difficulty remembering the sequence of events and hoped that a scroll and pen would be available to write down their agreements. In the future there would be many who might write down the words of Jesus and his followers; this request was the only one that would record an orderly record of what he did.

The Beginning of the Gospel

In the morning when he brought the tray of bread with honey, cheese and figs, John also brought his scroll and pen to begin what none of them understood as a document of eternal importance. He listened only to Simon when there was some dispute. It was a practical if sometimes noisy process. John wrote:

    Nazareth, John the baptizer and the desert temptations as reported by Jesus;
      Galilee:
           Call of the first four disciples
           Miracles in Capernaum
           Tour of Galilee
           Ministry in Capernaum
           Sabbath controversy
           Selection of the other eight disciples
           Teaching in Capernaum
           Parables of the Kingdom
           Crossing the Sea of Galilee
           Galilean miracles
           Unbelief in Nazareth
           Six teams tour Galilee
           King Herod's reaction
    Withdrawal from Galilee
           Eastern shore of Sea of Galilee
           Western shore of Sea of Galilee
           Phoenicia
           Decapolis
           Vicinity of Caesarea Philippi

Final ministry in Galilee
Teaching in Judea and Perea
> Concerning divorce
> Concerning children
> Rich young man
> Prediction of Jesus' death
> Request of James and John
> Miracle of Bartimaeus' sight
Final days:
> Jerusalem
>> Triumphal entry
>> Cleansing the Temple
>> Controversy with Jewish Leaders
>> Olivet discourse concerning the end of the age
> Bethany
>> Anointing Jesus
> Jerusalem Pass……..

He was interrupted by two women who burst into the terrace. One was Mary Magdalene, and the other was Mary the mother of James. With Salome, they had gone to the tomb to finish the burial of Jesus. They reported that the large stone was rolled away from the entrance, and inside they found a young man dressed in white who told them not to be alarmed; he knew they were looking for Jesus the Nazarene. The man told them, "He is risen! He is not here. Go tell his disciples and Peter."

Verification

Simon and the follower called John jumped up. If they had run away in the Garden, they were not about to show fear in this day. They both ran on a mission of discovery. It was after the ninth hour when they returned. The sun was casting afternoon shadows.

Simon said, "We both went in and saw the empty tomb. The cloths were folded, but there was no one there."

Everyone seemed to have something to say about that, even when John, the brother of James, reminded them that Jesus had told them beforehand what would happen to him and how on the third day he would be raised. When the voices became boisterous, Simon reminded them that there were guards patrolling the streets looking for them. An obedient hush brought the room back to order.

"Brothers," his voice was firm, "there is a deep mystery here. I think we must be in prayer until the Master shows us the way to it."

When Joseph and John delivered a tray of bread and cheese with a pitcher of watered wine, Andrew said, "I recall how he took the bread and said 'This is my body, broken for you,' and he took a blessing cup and said, 'Whoever eats this bread and drinks this wine will do it in remembrance of me.'" The group was in quiet worship as darkness took over the city.

Two breathless men from Emmaus entered the terrace, reporting that while they were making their way home a stranger joined their journey.

"He explained the scriptures in a most insightful way," they said, "but we didn't recognize him. When we were about to turn into our home, it seemed he was going further. We invited him to share our meal, and as he broke the bread, gave thanks and blessed it, we knew who he was. It was Jesus! Our hearts were burning with joy. Then he disappeared from our sight."

Now the conversations began again at that loud pitch.

Suddenly, Jesus was standing amidst them, and said, *"Peace be with you."* The terrace was shocked and silent, many thinking they were seeing a ghost.

"Why are you troubled?" Jesus asked. *"Why do doubts rise in your mind? Look at my hands and my feet. Touch me and see."*

He said to them, *"This is what I told you while I was still with you: 'Everything must be fulfilled that is written about me in the Law of Moses, the Prophets and the Psalms.'"* Then he opened their minds so they could understand the scriptures. He told them, *"This is what is written: 'The Christ will suffer and rise from the dead on the third day, and repentance and forgiveness of sins will be preached in his name to all nations, beginning at Jerusalem.' You are witnesses of these things. I am going to send you what my Father has promised; but stay in the city until you have been clothed with power from on high."* (Luke 24:36 ff.) He lifted up his hand and blessed them, and as suddenly as he had appeared to them he was taken up to heaven.

New Life, New Joy

Then they worshipped him into the night with great joy. John couldn't recall a happier, more hopeful time. He was included into this band of followers who had received a promise from Jesus. He had a task, a massive holy task to record these amazing events for the future. A process was forming into a workable plan to accomplish the task, if they just had time enough to do it. When he was no longer able to sing with them, or praise God with holy words, he knew he needed rest, but he promised Simon that he would return by the first hour with food and a writing page.

The long morning rays of sun were warming the terrace after worship and a bit of food. The followers were lounging around the table when John asked Simon to tell him how it had all started.

"After John, who had baptized Jesus, was put in prison, Jesus went about Galilee proclaiming the good news of God. 'The time has come,' he said, "The kingdom of God is near. Repent and believe the good news.' As he walked beside the Sea of Galilee, he saw Andrew and me casting our nets. All he said to us was 'Come follow me, and I'll make you fishers of men.' We left the nets at once, and followed him. A bit farther he saw, James, son of Zebedee, and his brother John, preparing to go out in their father's fishing boat. Immediately he called them and they left their father in the boat with the hired men, and followed him."

Simon thought for a moment, then continued, "As soon as he entered Capernaum, he came to our house; my mother-in-law was in bed with a high fever. We told Jesus about her..."

Andrew interrupted Simon, reminding him of the healing in the synagogue.

"You are right, brother. On the Sabbath Jesus went into our synagogue and began to teach as one who had authority, not as a teacher of the law. A man who was possessed by an evil spirit shouted, 'What do you want with us, Jesus of Nazareth? Have you come to destroy us? I know who you are – the Holy One of God!'"

"Jesus told the man to be quiet, and then commanded the evil spirit to come out of him. It shook the man violently and then came out with a shriek. The people were all amazed. They asked each other if this might be a new teaching. They said, 'He gives orders to evil spirits and they obey him.' That news spread quickly over the whole region."

Simon broke into a wide smile, "Now back to my mother-in-law; when Jesus heard about her illness, he went in to see her. He took her hand and helped her up. The fever left her, and she began to give us hospitality. That evening after sunset, the people brought to Jesus all the sick and demon-possessed. The whole town gathered at our door, and Jesus healed many with various ailments. He drove out many demons but would not let them speak because they knew who he was.

"Early the next morning Jesus went off to a solitary place to pray. When we finally found him we told him that the town was once again seeking him. Jesus bade us to go to another village nearby so he could preach there. He said that was the reason for his presence."

Andrew said quietly, "I recall how he healed a man with leprosy, who knelt before him and said, 'If you are willing, you can make me clean.' With compassion, Jesus simply said, 'I am willing. Be clean.' Immediately the leprosy left him and he was cured. Then Jesus sternly told the man to tell no one about this but to show himself to the priest and offer the sacrifices Moses had commanded. Instead the man went out and began to tell everyone. As a result Jesus could not enter a town openly but stayed out in the lonely places. But people still came to him from everywhere."

Thomas asked, "Do you recall what happened when we returned to Capernaum? The people came in droves. There were so many crowded around the house there was no way anyone else could get in. Four friends brought a paralytic on his mat. When they saw there was no other way to Jesus, they carried him up onto the roof where they made an opening and lowered him down. When Jesus saw their faith, he said to the paralytic, 'Son, your sins are forgiven.' But the religious teachers of the law who were there were thinking to themselves that only God can forgive sins, said 'This must be blaspheming!'

"Jesus immediately knew in his spirit what they were thinking. He asked them, 'Why are you thinking these things? Which is easier: to say to the paralytic, 'Your sins are forgiven, or to say, 'Get up, take your mat, and walk?' But that you may know that the Son of Man has authority on earth to forgive sins,' Jesus looked right at the man lying in front of him and said, 'I tell you, get up, take your mat, and go home.' The man got up, took his mat and walked out in full view of them all. This amazed everyone, and they praised God saying, 'We have never seen anything like this.'"

Matthew said with a sigh, "All that took place just before he called me."

Simon agreed. "He was walking again beside the lake with a crowd listening as he taught. When he saw you sitting in the tax booth he said, 'Follow me,' and you got up and followed him."

Matthew added, "That evening we were eating dinner in my house, and many tax collectors and sinners were there. When the teachers of the law who were Pharisees saw him eating with the sinners and tax collectors, they asked us, 'Why does he eat with tax collectors and sinners?' When Jesus heard that he told them, 'It is not the healthy who need a doctor, but the sick. I have not come to call the righteous, but sinners.'"

Names

Simon looked at John and said, "This reminds me to explain some of our names. There are two of us that Jesus called named Simon. I have believed he called me Peter, not because my faith is solid as a rock, but to help him tell us apart. Levi is called Matthew, perhaps to avoid the taint of historic reputation. James, the son of Zebedee, is sometimes confused with James the Less, son of Alpheus. And to avoid confusion, I'd like to call you John Mark, son of Silvanus to avoid confusion with the other son of Zebedee."

"You are adjusting my name so I may become part of the followers. I'm honored and delighted," the young man answered. "And if we can do tomorrow what we were able to do today, I will soon have the script of your entire journey with Jesus on a scroll. I feel I was called to this assignment."

The Scroll

Just that simply the process was established. Each morning at the first hour, John Mark would carry a tray of food and a pitcher of water to the terrace. The table was ringed with men whose collective memories were warm with the experiences they had but could never completely understand, stories of healings, lessons of redemption and forgiveness. They would talk, and John Mark would take accurate notes for three hours. At the third hour he would take his notes to his room and transfer them to his growing scroll. He was careful with the compilation of memories and had to warn himself not to get swept away with the wonder of it all.

After the sixth hour, the followers would make their way into the Temple, where in a side porch they would retell the accounts of Jesus. They were faithful to remember that he had directed them to preach repentance and forgiveness of sins, for the kingdom of God was at hand.

One morning the strength of their process was demonstrated. Peter had just told the account of Jesus healing the little girl, taking her hand and saying, "'Talitha koum,' and immediately she stood up and walked around. Then he sent us out in teams of two with authority to cast out evil spirits. These were his instructions."

Before he could say more, Thomas asked "Wasn't the visit to Nazareth before that? Remember how the people murmured, 'What's this wisdom that has been given to him that he even does miracles?' 'Isn't this Mary's son and these his family?' And they took offense at him."

James nodded and Thomas said, "Jesus said to them, 'Only in his own hometown among his relatives and his own house is a prophet without honor.' He could do no miracles there except lay hands on a few sick people and heal them. And he was amazed at their lack of faith."

"You're right," Peter affirmed, "and then he sent us out in teams of two. He said to us, 'Take nothing for the journey except a staff – no bread, no bag, no money in your belts. Wear sandals but not an extra tunic. Whenever you enter a house, stay there until you leave the town. And if any place will not welcome you or listen to you, shake the dust off your feet when you leave as a testimony against them.' We went out and preached that people should repent. We drove out many demons and anointed many sick people with oil and healed them." A smile spread across his face with the fond memory.

From across the table Andrew added, "That's about the time that King Herod heard about Jesus, for his name was becoming well known. Some were saying, 'John the Baptist has been raised from the dead, and that's why miraculous powers are at work in him.' Others said, 'He's Elijah.' And still others claimed, 'He is a prophet, like one of the prophets of long ago.' But when Herod heard this, he said, 'John, the man I beheaded, has been raised from the dead!'" Then they shared again the familiar story of Herod's party; Herodias, his wife and former wife of his brother Philip; and the dancing daughter who so aroused Herod that he pledged half his kingdom. All the while the busy pen of John Mark was recording the vivid memories of the men whose spirits were alive with joy.

Another Sabbath came and went, then another and another. Soon it would be the Festival of Weeks and John Mark felt it was nearing the time for his father's return.

Pentecost

It was the seventh Sabbath after another Passover. John's mother asked him to spread the invitation among the followers that there would be an abundance of bread, fruit, cheese, wine and honey for the Festival of Weeks tomorrow. In their daily visit to the Temple they were welcome to invite as many pilgrims as room allowed. Once again the city was filled to overflowing with those who made the long journey to celebrate the first fruits of the wheat harvest, and to recall with gratitude the covenant established on Mt. Sinai.

When John Mark passed along that invitation, he put more definite limitations, wanting to avoid too many or too few guests. "Today at the Temple, we may each invite four pilgrims to join us for the sixth hour meal tomorrow. That will snugly fill the house and enable mother to plan enough food for us all."

One of the followers said, "This house has been extremely generous with hospitality, and tomorrow will be a great example. Jesus told us to wait in the city until we receive the power God has prepared for us. I believe our period of waiting is nearly over. Please thank your mother again for her patience and generosity."

In the morning when he took the tray of food to the terrace, there was much laughter and teasing.

"John Mark, your legs are going to be as strong as a gazelle's. You have been up and down these stairs every day for weeks!"

"Your mother must be the proudest mother in Jerusalem with twelve hungry sons to feed each day!"

Finally Peter said, "I believe our recollections are drawing to a close, for we are recalling Jericho and Bethany before we came to Jerusalem. There was the account of Zachaeus and his tree perch as well as blind Bartimaeus. We are pretty sure you can see the finality of our journey now. There is so much to tell, and so little time now to tell it." None of them had any understanding of the truth just spoken.

On their return from the Temple, each with a quartet of grateful pilgrims, the followers were a tide of joyful anticipation. When they filled the house, Mary asked them to be seated at the table and all the rest to be comfortable on the floor. John Mark stood near the kitchen wall as he welcomed them all. He reminded them, "While we come from different towns and places, we may speak languages that are unknown to some, we all bear the promise that God will be our God, and we can be His people. This day reminds us that God provides abundance which makes us strong, and He provides a covenant that makes us a mighty nation."

Mary, standing near the kitchen door, began a familiar song: "On the holy mount stands the city founded; the Lord loves the gates of Zion more than the dwelling places of Jacob. Glorious things are spoken of you, O city of God." The tune repeated. Then she sang another that they all knew: "Steadfast love and faithfulness will meet; righteousness and peace will kiss each other. Faithfulness will spring up from the ground, and righteousness will look down from the sky. Yea, the Lord will give what is good, and our land will yield its increase. Righteousness will go before him, and make his footsteps a way." The refrain was repeated.

Then the servants brought out the trays of food and pitchers of wine. As they were emptied, new ones took their place. There was enough food for each person to have his fill.

At first the room was quiet with the welcome munching of food. After a bit conversations began as you might expect. Strangers were sharing their hearts and thanksgiving. For those far from their own home, this was a moment of powerful appreciation.

The sound was unheard at first, just a whisper amidst the chatter. But it grew louder, and louder still. Speaking stopped as they listened to a sound unlike anything they had ever heard, like a mighty wind. Suddenly there was with the sound lights, like tongues of flame that swirled and then came to rest over each man there. Someone shouted, "Behold, the Lord God comes with might," and all the other voices joined him saying, "Behold his reward is with him, and his recompense before him." And they could not control the shouts of joy and praise. They were all standing and embracing each other and praising God in their own languages, which they recognized and understood.

Finally Peter said, "This must be God's power, the gift Jesus said was prepared for us. Let's hurry back to the Temple and share this marvelous thing." They were in such a hurry to leave they overlooked the courtesy of thanking their hosts. Mary understood for she too was shaken by the wonder of it. She looked at John Mark for a long moment before saying, "I believe everything is about to change."

Spiritual power

The group of excited men found a side room already pretty filled with pilgrims. Andrew was leading them in a spirited song and soon had the attention of most in the porch. In a bold voice Simon Peter said, "This is what was spoken by the prophet Joel: 'In the last days, God says, I will pour out my spirit on all people. Your sons and daughters will prophesy, your young men will see visions, your old men will dream dreams. Even on my servants, both men and women, I will pour out my Spirit in those days, and they will prophesy. I will show wonders in heaven above, and signs on the earth below, blood and fire and billows of smoke. The sun will be turned to darkness and the moon to blood before the coming of the great and glorious day of the Lord. And everyone who calls on the name of the Lord will be saved.'" Many who were standing nearby gave him their attention.

"Men of Israel," his voice grew stronger, "listen to this: Jesus of Nazareth was a man accredited by God to you by miracles, wonders and signs, which God did among you through him, as you yourselves know. This man was handed over to you by God's set purpose and knowledge; and you, with the help of wicked men, put him to death by nailing him to the cross. But God raised him from the dead, freeing him from the agony of death, because it was impossible for death to keep its hold on him. David said about him: 'I saw the Lord always before me. Because he is at my right hand, I will not be shaken. Therefore my heart is glad and my tongue rejoices; my body will live in hope, because you will not abandon me to the grave, nor will you let your Holy One see decay. You have made known to me the paths of life; you will fill me with joy in your presence.'

"Brothers, I can tell you confidently that the patriarch David died and was buried and his tomb are here to this day. But he was a prophet and knew that God had promised him on oath that he would place one of his descendants on his throne. Seeing what was ahead, he spoke of the resurrection of the Christ, that he was not abandoned to the grave, nor did his body see decay. God has raised this Jesus to life, and we are all witnesses of the fact. Exalted to the right hand of God, he has received from the Father the promised Holy Spirit and has poured out what you now see and hear. For David did not ascend to heaven, and yet he said, 'The Lord said to my Lord: Sit at my right hand until I make your enemies a footstool for your feet.' Therefore let all Israel be assured of this: God has made this Jesus, whom you crucified, both Lord and Christ."

As those words were understood, the crowd became solemn and still. The heavy awareness of guilt held them in a powerful grip. Someone near the back called out in anguish, "Brothers, what shall we do?"

Peter responded, boldly, "Repent and be baptized, every one of you, in the name of Jesus Christ for the forgiveness of your sins. And you will receive the gift of the Holy Spirit. The promise is for you and your children and for all who are far off – for all whom the Lord our God will call." He spoke passionately, pleading for them to save themselves from this corrupt generation.

The effect on the crowd was amazing. As many as three thousand responded, receiving baptism and fresh hope.

John Mark was astonished at what he was witnessing. He could scarcely contain his joy. He was watching a new era of fellowship forming among these people. There was generosity and prayer; there was encouragement and eager excitement to hear more from the followers. He ran home to tell his mother what a powerful thing had happened.

Her genuine smile was encouraging him to share more of what he had seen.

"And then Peter laid upon them the awesome guilt of crucifying Jesus. You could hear voices from the Gentile Court, but not a whisper from our porch. When Simon told them to repent of their sins and receive forgiveness and the Holy Spirit, it was like a storm of believers that surrounded the followers. There was that same noise that we heard here in the house as everyone was praising together. I really hope the followers will talk about this day when they come back here for the evening. Perhaps I can hear them, and learn more."

"You are a good student, John Mark. How is the progress on your scroll coming along?" Her affectionate smile made him glad.

"It's a very large task. I have many notes that are waiting their turn. Things seem to be happening that are very important to include. Peter believes I can now see the conclusion, but I feel like we are simply standing at the beginning of a very large story that will bring a huge change."

Her smile changed to one of inquiry. "Do you mean change for you, or our family?"

"I'm too young to be wise, but I do believe the change will be for us all. Some of the things of the past will lose their value, and new horizons of wonder will call us away. The followers seem to have no roots, yet they are quite content, even fearless, talking about Jesus. My heart races when I am with them. I believe there is much, much more to this story."

Resistance

The truth of his words was made evident a couple days later when Peter and John were once again entering the Temple. It was the ninth hour and still a crippled man was begging by the entrance. He called out, "Alms for the poor," as he had countless times before. If he was weary of his birth plight, he was more weary of the blind eyes that refused him any assistance.

"Alms, alms for the poor", his small voice called out to the large crowd.

Peter stopped and told the man to look at them. He told the crippled man, "I don't have money for you, but what I do have I give you: in the name of Jesus Christ of Nazareth, walk." Peter took the man's right hand and helped him stand. Immediately the man's feet and legs were strengthened. He was able to walk and jump with joy. Praising God he went with them into the Temple where many who had witnessed the wonder gathered around him, amazed at what had just occurred.

Once again Peter took advantage of the moment by making clear to them that this man had not been healed by their power or godliness. "The God of Abraham, Isaac, and Jacob, the God of our fathers has glorified his servant Jesus." Once again he explained how the night of injustice had been followed by the day of the cross and their role in it.

"You killed the author of life, but God raised him from the dead. We are witnesses of this. By faith in the name of Jesus, this man whom you see and know was made strong. It is Jesus' name and the faith that comes through him that has given this complete healing to him, as you can all see." He preached to them and called for repentance, with the promise of forgiveness and the Holy Spirit.

A group of the temple priests accompanied by some Sadducees, along with the captain of the temple guard approached while Peter was still speaking. The angry group was disturbed by the content of their teaching, primarily that they proclaimed Jesus' resurrection of the dead, and they were envious of the large crowd's response. The guards roughly seized Peter and John. Since it was almost evening, they would be jailed until the Sanhedrin could hear them in the morning. That judicial body, Israel's Supreme Court, was made up of three groups, rulers, elders, and teachers of the law, one of whom was a young Pharisee named Saul, of Tarsus. John Mark wept as he left the temple feeling overwhelmed with his powerlessness to assist his friends. It was, after all, the Sanhedrin that had condemned Jesus to death.

As he approached his home, John Mark heard the sound of singing coming from the terrace. The followers were joined in worship, giving God thanks for the wonder of this day. The young man hurried to join them, for he was mystified at their response. James was saying, "Jesus did not promise us comfort, but tribulation. Don't you recall how he said, 'In the world you will have tribulation, but be of good cheer, I have overcome the world.'?" There was nodding in agreement. "These men are driven by popularity of the crowd. Those who saw the wonder of the beggar's healing will not allow anything hurtful to happen to Simon or my brother, even though the priests may want that. This is a time for us to do as Jesus directed us: remember when he said, 'Let not your hearts be troubled, neither let them be afraid.' Let us all join in giving God praise for the wonder that is happening in the name of Jesus, the Christ." Once again the voices joined in a song of devotion.

John Mark turned around and descended the stairs, smiling with new insight. The faith of these men was pushing back the shadows of dread. He realized that grieving in advance was a toy of the Tempter. If James was correct, the arrest of Peter and John might turn out to be another surprise opportunity.

It was just after the sixth hour prayers the next day that Peter and John returned hungry but filled with joy. They were exuberant with confidence, for the support of the crowd and the presence of an obviously healed beggar had kept the priests from doing harm to Peter or John. Between eager bites of food they told of their arrest and appearing before the Sanhedrin.

"They would have loved nothing more than to silence us forever, but the people murmured against them," John said.

Peter added, "They sent us out so they could confer what to do. When they brought us back in, they commanded us to neither teach nor preach in the name of Jesus." John leaned over and finished the thought, "Peter told them to judge for themselves whether it was right to obey the counsel rather than God. For we cannot help speaking about what we have seen and heard. There was nothing they could do but scold us with threats and let us go." The terrace became hushed in prayer as all the followers knelt giving the Redeemer praise. Suddenly the house was shaken, and they were all filled with the Holy Spirit. To each one there was a new resolve to tell of the wonders they were seeing.

Perhaps Joseph was anticipating the needs of the followers who were talking about expanding their area of witness, or perhaps he was simply caught up in the glorious moment. He sold a field he owned in Cyprus, and presented the money to the apostles. Some had been calling him Barnabas, which means "son of encouragement," but now all did. It was another opportunity to express resolve.

Now a man named Ananias also owned a field, which he could sell. Perhaps it was the love of praise that caused him to want to donate the money to the followers, but it may have been the love of money that caused him to keep some of it for himself. Had he been forthright with the apostles there would have been no problem. But when he presented the money to them, with the full knowledge of Sapphira his wife, attesting it as the total from the sale, Peter confronted him of the deception. The man fell down, seized by great fear, and died. Three hours later, when his wife heard of it, she also collapsed and died. All who saw it were shocked with awe.

Arrested Again

Day after day the apostles were in the temple, preaching their faith in the name of Jesus and healing many of their illnesses. Crowds gathered from the towns around Jerusalem, bringing their sick and those tormented by evil spirits, and all were healed. So once again, the High Priest and all his associates who were members of the party of the Sadducees, were filled with jealousy and had them once again arrested and placed in jail. During the night, however, an angel of the Lord opened the doors of the jail and brought them out.

"Go, stand in the temple court," he told them, "and tell the people the full message of this new life."

In the morning when the Sanhedrin gathered the full assembly of elders of Israel, they sent to the jail for the apostles. But they had to report that the jail was empty, and they were told the apostles were yet again speaking to the crowd in Solomon's porch in the temple. The captain of the guard went with his officers and seized the apostles, but they did not use force because they feared the attentive crowd would resist them.

The angry High Priest said to Peter, "We gave you strict orders not to teach in this name. Yet you have filled Jerusalem with your teaching and are determined to make us guilty of this man's blood."

Peter and the other apostles replied, "We must obey God rather than men! The God of our fathers raised Jesus from the dead – whom you killed by hanging him on a tree. God exalted him to his own right hand as Prince and Savior that he might give repentance and forgiveness of sins to Israel. We are witnesses of these things, and so is the Holy Spirit, whom God has given to those who obey him."

Now the Sanhedrin was furious! Angry voices were shouting for the death of these men. After a few moments of chaos, a calm voice gained control. It was Gamaliel, a teacher of the law. In fact, there were many, including a young Pharisee by the name of Saul of Tarsus, who believed he was The Teacher of the law. Gamaliel called for the trouble makers to be removed from the room to defuse the moment. When they were finally quiet, he said, "Men of Israel, consider carefully what you intend to do to these men." Then he reminded the court of other distractions that had occurred, when dynamic leaders raised a following. "But when the leader was killed, the followers dispersed, and it all came to nothing. Therefore, in this present case, I advise you to leave these men alone. Let them go! For if their purpose or activity is of human origin, it will fail. But if it is from God, you will not be able to stop these men; you will only find yourselves fighting against God." There were several who still believed the crime was too extreme to overlook.

The High Priest called the apostles back in and had them flogged. Their bloody backs were an appeasement for those who had called for a more severe punishment. The apostles were ordered not to speak in the name of Jesus, and they were released. All the way back to the terrace they rejoiced because they had been found worthy of suffering disgrace for the Name. Day after day, in the temple courts and from house to house, they never stopped teaching and proclaiming the good news that Jesus is the Christ.

A Different Report

When Silvanus returned from the northern principalities he found great change, in Jerusalem, and especially in his own home. The legate was overjoyed at the successful tax gathering. There had been only four properties confiscated for unpaid taxes, and six sent to the dungeon.

"That positive report, however, is negated," according to the spokesman for the governor, "by a Passover incident that was most unsettling. A pilgrim who was using the terrace of your home committed an offense so heinous that the temple guard was called out at night to raid the house. When the man fled into Gethsemane, they followed and arrested him. It was a dreadful night for the governor," the legate shuddered. "There were hours of political maneuvering. Finally Governor Pilate had no other recourse but to sentence the man to death with two other criminals. The whole thing was so avoidable. Of course he does not blame you. On the other hand, he is looking for some place to place responsibility, and you are at the top of his list. He abhors conflict. My suggestion to you is that you stay far from his attention. It would be a good idea if you allow no one the use of your home for a few years. Perhaps he will forgive you."

"But that is so unreasonable," Silvanus said softly. "I had nothing to do with the man or his conduct in Jerusalem."

"Perhaps not." The legate appeared bored with the conversation. "'Where there is smoke,' as they say. I'm afraid a most unfavorable political wind is blowing on you right now. Because of your excellent work in the past, I will try to keep your status for the future. But as I say, it will be wise of you to stay out of the governor's attention."

Conflicting Loyalties

Silvanus' homecoming was far different. As usual, Mary welcomed him back from his journey as a beloved spouse. Her embrace and kiss left him a bit breathless. Then she began to pour out the events since Passover. John Mark joined her, adding much of his own insight to the activity of the followers. Perhaps the most obvious detail for Silvanus to comprehend was the number of men still staying in the terrace. That had become the staging for the temple visits as well as the door to door activity. It was a place of almost constant prayer and worship. Mary explained that recent charitable gifts to them made it possible for them to compensate her for their food and a bit for lodging, so they were still paying guests. Then he told her of the conversation with the legate, and the recommendation to allow no one use of the terrace.

"When you have a chance to feel their conviction and joy, I think you will not worry about the legate." Mary told him with a smile. "There is something very wonderful going on here."

When John Mark showed him the scroll that he was still completing, Silvanus realized just how true her words had been. There was something beyond explanation here. It only took a short while before he knew he wanted to be a part of it as well.

Stephen

One of the new additions to the followers was a handsome young man named Stephen. He was eager to be involved, and his intelligence and eloquence quickly set him as a leader. He was asked to care for the needs of the Greek widows in the daily distribution of food, a task he gladly accepted. He also had opportunities to speak in the temple porch, and his abilities came to the attention of those beyond the faith who were jealous of him. They tried to engage him in debate but could not equal his knowledge or clarity. So they fabricated an accusation that he had uttered blasphemy against Moses and against God.

Everything might have remained manageable had Stephen not been so aware of his own innocence or so filled with the spirit of righteousness. If he had not chosen to relate all the sins of the past to this Sanhedrin; if he had not chosen to give them an opportunity to acknowledge their sinfulness, he might have had a chance. But he didn't have a chance of a peaceful outcome when he said, "You stiff-necked people, with uncircumcised hearts and ears! You are just like your fathers: You always resist the Holy Spirit! Was there ever a prophet your fathers did not persecute? They even killed those who predicted the coming of the righteous One. And now you have betrayed and murdered him, you who have received the law that was put into effect through angels but have not obeyed it!" No, he didn't have a chance. Their fury spilled into raw rage and they dragged him out of the city and stoned him.

Stephen prayed, "Lord Jesus, receive my spirit." He fell to his knees, and cried out, "Lord, do not hold this sin against them." He fell under the barrage of their hate. And Saul of Tarsus was there giving approval to his death.

On that day a terrible persecution broke out against the church at Jerusalem, and all the followers were scattered throughout Judea and Samaria. Saul began to destroy the church, and he started where they were most likely to be, in the terrace at the home of Silvanus.

The evening meal was just being shared when the door burst open, and the family could hear heavy footsteps pounding up the outside stairway. The terrace was vacant, and only the family was seated at the table. Silvanus stood and confronted the angry temple guards.

"Stop, now!" he commanded. "You are far outside your duties! Or would you like to face my Roman century?" That caught their attention. They stood still, but were still surly.

"We are seeking the followers of Jesus, Greek. Who are you?"

"I am owner of this house, and Tax Consul for Governor Pilate. I have only in the past few days returned from a six month obligation with my Roman guard. I don't want to know who you are, but if you don't leave immediately we will see how red Jewish blood really is." His voice was calm but deathly cold. Those standing nearest the broken door began to back out.

Looking at John Mark, the short Pharisee asked loudly, "Where did they go?"

The young man was startled but answered immediately, "I think they said they were going back to Galilee."

"Enough of this," Silvanus said much more firmly. "Leave now or face the consequences." All these Jews understood that a Greek in charge of a Roman Century would not hesitate putting them on a cross, just for publicity.

The Pharisee postured a bit, but was also wisely heading for the doorway. "We will root you out like vermin if we find you are with them." But he was sort of scooting as he said it.

The Persecution Grows

In the following days and weeks Saul of Tarsus arrested many, sending them to prison, and scattering the other believers well beyond Jerusalem's walls. James, John, and Andrew went back to Capernaum. Simon Peter went to Joppa before rejoining them. Matthew went to Jericho, Philip went into Samaria, and the rest found safety outside the city. They all continued to teach and preach in the name of Jesus, and wondrous signs accompanied them all.

Silvanus made his way through the early morning, past the High Priest's house, then the open Theater. Here in the center of the city the heat of the summer sun made the air heavy to breathe, or perhaps it was the required audience with the legate that made the air so still. The walls along the street seemed closer and more impenetrable in the Upper City. He was led through a gate, across a courtyard, and into an ante room where he was told to wait.

Nearly an hour went by before the legate's assistant told Silvanus that he would be seen now. He was directed to a large room with a small table. The legate sat in the only chair; obviously this was not a cordial appointment.

"I believe I told you to remain out of Pilot's attention," he began the serious conversation. "Your house was the scene of yet another riot, Silvanus. The temple guards were called to quiet it." The baseless words were whispered in a disgusted voice.

"Sir, there was no riot," Silvanus said in defense. "The guards were searching for the same men who had stayed in the rooftop terrace. They had left the city before the guards arrived."

"Those are simply details," the unpleasant man said softly. "The sad point is that you failed to heed my warning, and now the governor wants a new Tax Consol for the northern provinces. Your time here is at an end. Procorus of Gadara, a Roman without a Hebrew wife, will take your place by the autumn equinox. He lives in a profitable vineyard, and we have determined that it is about the same value as your comfortable home. I am proposing that you simply exchange homes, unless of course, you would prefer to find some other lodging. In either event, Procorus will move into your present house." The legate expected some sort of outburst or some sign of contrition.

After a lengthy silence, the standing man responded. "I am truly sorry for this misconception, sir," Silvanus said pleasantly. "But I will not be sorry to share the time I have left with my son and wife. I believe there have been too many springs that I have apologized to them for my absence. We will begin today to make arrangements. You are correct; I didn't heed the warning and must now pay the consequences. Perhaps I may even learn to run a vineyard." He turned and walked to the door, but not downcast as the legate had anticipated. In fact, there may have even been a bit of relief in his straight back and firm steps.

Another Confirmation Class

The confirmation class had cleaned up the platter of doughnuts. Jerry waited until the last to make sure everyone who wanted a chocolate one had a choice, then he took the last one left. Pastor Randle had told them there were only two sessions remaining. He had asked them in preparation for this class to draw a picture of their idea of what he meant when he said, "church." Jerry could see that some had spent some time with their drawing, and others had been in a hurry to get it done. They went around the circle explaining what they had drawn.

"Good job, ya'll," Mr. Randle said in his favorite Southern drawl. "You can see how the word 'church' can mean a lot of different things Way back in history the Latin word that we started with was 'ekklesia.' It came from two parts; 'ek' which means 'out' and kaleo' which means 'to call.'"

Shelly raised her hand and asked, "Is that like the book from the fourth shelf of the old part, Ecclesiastes?"

"Super question!" the teacher complimented. "In Hebrew that means 'chosen assembly.' In the scriptures of the New Testament, 'church' always referred to a gathering of people that met in a synagogue or someone's home, or in the open, like where they gathered at the river to do their laundry. There's just one more word I want to tell you about today, and then we'll get to an important list. Our word 'church' with a little 'c' means the whole or universal church, all churches. If we use a capital 'C', it refers to the Roman Catholic Church, which was the only church for almost a thousand years. The Orthodox church was a part of it that was formed in Egypt and grew in central Europe. Next week we will look at the reformed churches.

A New Home Together

y, John Mark's mother was quite upset when Silvanus shared
s of his dismissal. She had so many friends here in Jerusalem,
s house was the center of such uplifting fellowship. She wept
her sense of loss.

'It has also become the target for the High Priest's henchmen
king believers. We have become a danger for those brave friends,"
vanus explained. "I believe there will be new friends in Gadara, and
safe opportunity to expand the work of the followers." He stretched
his arms wide, nearly shouting, "And we will be winemakers, together,
all year long!"

John Mark tried to match his father's enthusiasm. "If I can't find
a use for my script taking, I will be glad to be a winemaker. It is a
most honorable occupation. Perhaps we can even have a few goats
and make cheese as well."

Still whimpering, Mary said sadly, "But Gadara is in the province
of Decapolis, the region of Ten Towns." Her opinion of the region was
in her sad tone of voice.

"All the safer for our friends, with more than enough room to
become another center of faith, and it is only a three day journey from
here." Silvanus was not about to let his bright hope fade.

"Now the list I printed for you are the characteristics of the first
century church. Turn to the book of Acts, page 1022 of your study
Bibles. Got it? O.K. now turn to chapter 2, verse 42. I'll read slowly,
and you can either read with me or just listen. *'They devoted themselves
to the apostles' teaching and to the fellowship, to the breaking of bread and to
prayer. Everyone was filled with awe, and many wonders and miraculous signs
were done by the apostles. All the believers were together and had everything
in common. Selling their possessions and goods, they gave to anyone as he
had need. Every day they continued to meet together in the temple courts.
They broke bread in their homes and ate together with glad and sincere hearts,
praising God and enjoying the favor of all the people. And the Lord added to
their number daily those who were being saved.'*

"I've given you a list of nine qualities. As I go through the list,
see how many of them we have here in our own church. Place a
checkmark by them.

"The first characteristic was a learning church; they listened
intently to what the apostles taught. One of the dangers in the church
is that we might stop listening. Almost all of you have a smart phone
and know how fast technology is changing. But I'll bet that unless
your grandpa has had help, he can't maneuver around all your apps.
Things are changing rapidly. In the same way we should count it a
wasted day when we do not learn something new, or when we have
not penetrated more deeply into the wisdom and grace of God.

"The second characteristic was a church of fellowship. It had what
someone has called the great quality of togetherness. The sea captain
Lord Nelson once explained one of his great victories by saying,'I had
the happiness to command a band of brothers.' The church is only real
when it is a band of sisters and brothers.

"The third characteristic is it was a praying church. These early
followers knew that they could not meet life in their own strength
and they did not need to do so. They always spoke with God before
they spoke with others. They always went to God before they went

into the world. They could meet the problems of the world because they had first met with God.

"The fourth is they were a reverent church, which means they were awesome. It was said of a great believer that he moved through the world as though it were a temple. The believer lives in a reverence, awe, because he knows that the whole round world is the temple of the living God.

"The fifth is it was a church where things happened. Signs and wonders were not unusual. If we expect great things from God, and attempt great things for God, I guarantee great things are going to happen. More awesome things would happen if we believed that God and we, working together, could make them happen.

"Six, it was a sharing church, because the early followers had an intense feeling of responsibility for each other. You might be sad to hear that someone in Tibet has lost their home in an earthquake. But if it's your grandpa and grandma's house, you will for sure do all that you can to help them. A follower could not bear to have too much when others had too little.

"The seventh characteristic is it was a worshipping church. They never forgot the joy of visiting God's house. There are a lot of folks who log onto our live-stream each Sunday morning. I can't help making the comparison that they are like people who watch a televised football game instead of joining the thrill of the twelfth man by rooting or cheering for their team. Things happen when we gather together as one great body. The Spirit of God moves upon God's worshipping people.

"Which leads me to the eighth characteristic; it was a happy church. Gladness was there. A gloomy Christian is a contradiction of terms. It may not be a boisterous noisy thing, but deep down in the heart of a follower there is a joy that cannot be taken away.

"The last characteristic is a sum of all those other ones. It was a growing church of people others could only admire and like and want to be with. A real Christian is a lovely thing; they were winsome.

I had a Bible Professor name
enjoyed using the word 'bonni
all know folks whom we would c
the motions and present a nice fa
very loving. They are not bonnie, goo
church. A bonnie church is a growing

The confirmation class spent their las
their list and what it revealed to them abou

The Road to Damascus

Saul had finally found an adversary he could righteously pursue with abandon. He could still remember the heat of dragging Stephen out through the gate and surrounding him with their wrath. If he had not died so nobly, that memory would not keep him awake at night. His words still sighed through Saul's conscience, "Lord, do not hold this sin against them." But Saul hunted the believers all across the city. *(Acts 8:1) Wherever he could find them they were arrested and thrown into prison. He was convinced that he was satisfying the will of God, and would one day be hailed as the "Defender of Jerusalem."

By the time Silvanus and his family had met their new home, Saul had determined that the city was safe from the blasphemous plague. Damascus was a six day journey north, but since it was a center of commerce to the wider Syrian world, he felt if he could attack the uprising there, he could contain it finally. He walked ahead of the squad of temple guards who accompanied him; after all he was a noted Pharisee, and they were commoners.

They were nearing the city; soon it would be in sight. The sun was overhead when suddenly Saul was in the presence of a powerful bright light that knocked him to the ground. He clearly heard a voice ask, "*Saul, Saul, why do you persecute me?*"

"Who are you, Lord," the confused man asked, but was convinced he knew the answer.

"*I am Jesus, whom you are persecuting. Now get up and go into the city, and you will be told what you must do.*" The light was too powerful to ignore, and too clear to be misunderstood.

Saul staggered to his feet, but when he tried to open his eyes, there was only darkness. His hands thrashed about like someone lost. The guards had been mystified, for they had heard the sound, but there was no one to be seen. They took hold of the Pharisee's hand and led him into Damascus, where a believer by the name of Ananias was about to be surprised.

The Lord called to that gentle man in a vision. *"Ananias."*

"Yes, Lord." He answered obediently.

"Go to the house of Judas on Straight Street and ask for a man from Tarsus named Saul, for he is praying. In a vision he has seen a man named Ananias come and place his hand on him to restore his sight."

Ananias was hesitant, explaining that he had heard about this man and the harm he had caused to the believers in Jerusalem.

The instructions seemed to be non-negotiable, for the Lord said, *"Go! This man is my chosen instrument to carry my name before the Gentiles and their kings and before the people of Israel. I will show him how much he must suffer for my name."*

Perhaps cautiously, Ananias went to the house and entered it. Placing his hands on Saul, he said, "Brother Saul, the Lord – Jesus, who appeared to you on the road as you were coming here – has sent me so that you may see again and be filled with the Holy Spirit." Immediately, something like scales fell from Saul's eyes, and he could see again. He got up and was baptized, and after taking some food, the first in three days, he regained his strength.

The conversion of the man who set out on this journey to harm the believers, now shared his heart honestly with them that Jesus is truly the Son of God. Even those who knew of Saul's past and intent at coming here were amazed as he proved that Jesus is the Christ. Day after day he spoke in the synagogues with knowledge and personal experience, calling his listeners to repent of their sins and receive forgiveness and the Holy Spirit.

It only took a few weeks of that for the Jews, who had expected something far different from Saul, to become angry with his message. Finally they plotted his death and kept a strict watch on the city gates in order to kill him. Their plans were discovered, however, and followers, under the cloak of darkness, lowered Saul in a basket at an opening in the wall. He made his way back to Capernaum in the hopes of meeting with the apostles, only to be told that they had returned to Jerusalem months prior. He was directed to a vineyard near Gadara, where he might find a believer named Joseph. So it was that the pathway of Saul would eventually find a supportive heart.

Applied Conversion

Johanan, the vine dresser, knocked gently on the door. When Silvanus answered it, he was told that a certain man from Jerusalem would value a few moments of his time.

"Did he indicate what he might be seeking so far from home?" Silvanus asked.

"No, sir," the quiet man answered. "But he was polite for an educated man. I sense he is used to people obeying his commands. He seems to me as a man of authority."

"Invite him in. If he comes in peace, we will welcome him with hospitality." If Silvanus had known the identity of the visitor there might not have been such a gracious invitation, even though it was the kind thing to do.

When the two men were facing the open door, Silvanus said, "I remember the last time you burst into my house. Are the priests' thugs still with you?"

"Silvanus, I regret that meeting and pray that you might forgive my rudeness." The words were nearly shocking. Then Saul told Silvanus the account of being called by Jesus and healed of blindness by his Spirit and the hands of Ananias. He also told of preaching in Damascus until the Jews so opposed him.

"Sir, I am seeking Simon of Capernaum, who might introduce me to other leaders of the faith. I seek their forgiveness and blessing to be a part of this wonderful preaching ministry. In the vision Ananias had, God has selected me to be a light to the Gentiles, to bring the hope of God's love to those in far away homes. But I know I cannot do that alone. I must have the support and encouragement of the group."

Silvanus was silent for a long moment. "When we speak of God's unfailing forgiveness, it is humbling when we learn that his love is always greater than our ignorance. Saul, you are welcome to stay with us until you are rested enough to continue your journey. You spoke of encouragement. Here's a coincidence; my brother in law, Joseph, is still with us, and the apostles have begun calling him 'Barnabas,' for he is truly a son of encouragement. I am certain that when he hears of your desire to meet the men of Jerusalem, he will be glad to accompany you and lend his influence to introduce you and assure them that you are no longer a threat."

In Jerusalem it took a bit of searching before Joseph and Saul found Simon Peter in a porch of the temple. When he learned of Joseph's intention, Peter quickly protested. "That is the man who would have gladly arrested us all, and delivered us to prison." But after hearing Joseph's heartfelt account of Saul's encounter with Jesus, his healing and his assignment to proclaim the gospel to the Gentiles, Peter's resistance softened.

He told both Joseph and Saul the account that James, the brother of Jesus, had shared with them. "He said that at the scene of the cross, he had become aware of how wrong he had been not to accept his brother's invitation to accept God's forgiving grace. James had taken a Nazarite vow to never drink wine again until he could drink it with Jesus in paradise." Peter nodded his head in recollection of James' words. "He told us that the same day Jesus appeared to us on the terrace, he appeared to James, and offered him a cup of wine. He told his brother that he should drink this cup in remembrance of the forgiving blood shed for our sins." Peter was still for a bit, then looking at Saul he said, "It seems to me that it is good that the others have gone out to preach. You and James share a special uniqueness. You both were confronted by the Risen Lord and given a task. James is to help guide the followers here in Jerusalem." Then looking at Saul, he said, "And you are to speak to all, Jews and Gentiles, to help them find God's forgiveness." The strong man held out his hand in a gesture of greeting. "Welcome brother." He embraced Saul in a way that surprised the former Pharisee, but made him smile uncharacteristically.

Saul was free to move about Jerusalem, preaching boldly in the name of Jesus. He debated with the Grecian Jews so efficiently they decided to kill him. When the brothers learned about the plot, they took him to Caesarea and sent him off to Tarsus where he would be out of harm's grasp.

The Gospel Grows

The time of tranquility bloomed upon the fledgling fellowship. The apostles preached in the name of Jesus wherever they went with astounding success. Philip had great response in Samaria and Peter healed many as well. At Caesarea a centurion named Cornelius, a devout and generous man, had a vision that Peter was in Joppa. He sent two of his servants and one of his soldiers to go and invite Simon Peter to come stay in his house. At the same time Peter had a vision in the middle of the day that a sheet filled with all sorts of animals was lowered to him with the instructions to "kill and eat."

Peter's response was, "Surely not, Lord. I have never eaten anything impure or unclean."

The vision was repeated twice more, then the voice said, "Do not call anything impure that God has made clean."

He was still pondering the meaning of the vision when the men from Cornelius arrived. Even though it was clearly forbidden for a Jew to receive hospitality from a Gentile, he went with them along with several of the brothers. What they found there was a large gathering of people who had gladly received the teachings of Jesus. But when Peter began to preach to them about receiving forgiveness of their sins and the Holy Spirit, the reception was astonishing. They began praising God and speaking in tongues. Peter asked, "Can anyone keep these people from being baptized with water? They have received the Holy Spirit just as we have." It was a time of tranquility and growth.

The lamps were once again holding back the vineyard shadows of dusk as the men lingered at the table. There was much news to share. Silvanus had told Joseph and John Mark that this second grape harvest was outstanding. "There are many men of Gadara who look forward to earning wages as harvesters, and then pruners, so there is no shortage of eager workers. Johanan, the son of the original owner still has a room in the lower part of the winery where the aging jars are stored. He does all the wine, making for one percent of the production. This change has been a blessing for me. I have ample time to share the Gospel and still enjoy my family."

Joseph had shared briefly how Saul, a Pharisee hostile to the faith, had been met by Jesus on the road to Damascus and had eventually arrived to get Joseph's assistance to meet with the leaders. He had been so effective in proclaiming the Gospel in Jerusalem that the Jews had plotted to kill him, and James sent him to Tarsus for his safety.

Joseph said enthusiastically, "There was such astounding acceptance by the Gentiles in Antioch that James asked me to go there and see the wonder for myself. I realized that it was much more wide-spread than we had first heard, so I went to Tarsus to seek Saul's expertise." Joseph's happy smile was a sign of the victory he felt. "He has become known as 'Paul', which is a more Greek name. And speaking of names, I am becoming fond of my new name, 'Barnabas.'"

He continued in a happy voice, "The brothers in Antioch heard that a famine was gripping Judea. They took an offering to give assistance, and asked us to get it there as soon as possible." His voice became soft as he reflected on the other events,

"Before we were able to present the gift, Herod decided to persecute the believers of the Way. He arrested Peter, and had James, the brother of John, beheaded. The same terrible fate would have been Peter's, but an angel opened his chains and the doors to the prison. He escaped to Joppa. I expect you have heard of Herod's horrible death. Still, the people believe and the spread of the Gospel is inspiring."

Silvanus had listened to the account with great interest. Finally he asked, "What can I do to help? Could I add to the gift of mercy?"

"Much of our needs are already being cared for; you have offered us hospitality and a place to rest." Something of a new hope lit Barnabas' face as he continued. "But there is one other need we would share with you. Paul has need of a secretary to accompany us. He heard me sing the praise of John Mark's ability to record." Looking at John Mark, who had been quietly listening, he asked, "Have you completed the scroll for Peter?"

"Very nearly," the young man answered. "I have just finished the announcement of Jesus' resurrection." His voice softly added, "There is just the triumphant finish left on my notes. But I can finish it later." It was apparent to the men that he was eager to be part of their journey.

"But what about your work here in the vineyard?" Barnabas asked sincerely.

"I'm still a raw student," the young man replied with a shrug. "Next season or the one after that I can begin all over. I would be so very honored to accompany you." John Mark looked steadily into the eyes of each man, especially his father's.

Paul, who had been pretty quiet, observed, "He's very young to be on such a demanding journey. I agree we would benefit from a scribe, but such an inexperienced lad might be a liability to us."

Before Barnabas could answer, John Mark said softly, "I saw him arrested in Gethsemane. I recorded hours of the lessons and signs the apostles remembered from their years with Jesus. My heart thrilled at the wonder they shared. I was there on the terrace when the risen Christ appeared to us all, opening our minds to the scriptures and blessing us. How would you say that compares with your experience on the road to Damascus?" The level look he gave was not hostile, nor was it intimidated. For a long moment none of the other three had anything to say.

Finally Paul said with the closest he could come to a smile, "Forgive me. Of course you have a great deal to offer. The Pharisee in me has learned to overlook the quality of spirit in others all around me. In some ways my eyes are even yet blind. I must pray for further healing." He reached his hands across to touch John Mark's in a sign of conciliation, but it was not the end of distrust between them. ★(Acts 13:5)

Silvanus had watched the response from his son, assured now that he had a budding maturity. "The journey to Antioch will take you more than two weeks," he said to the three, "if you travel on land, but less than half that if you sail from Caesarea. I can provide contact to several ships I have used and passage for the three of you to Seleucia. Do you know how long you will be gone?" Grinning a disclaimer, he added, "His mother will be anxious during his absence."

"We will try to be faithful to the spirit's guidance." Barnabas thought out loud. "Our initial hope is to perhaps preach our way across Cyprus. There are many synagogues that would welcome us there. If we take advantage of the calm winter weather, we may be back here before the next harvest."

Missionary Journey Number One

The following morning Silvanus watched the three make their way out of the vineyard, and wondered if the tall lad would ever be a winemaker.

The Seleucia bound freighter they boarded had brought lumber to Caesarea and was going back filled with leather tents and bales of sheep hides. Paul had requested they spend as much time as possible on the forward peak of the ship, where the stench was lessened.

Barnabas smiled, saying, "I find the leather smell rather pleasant."

Paul grimaced, "My training was to avoid anything that was dead, unless it was kosher. I know that I have been set free from the law, but I'm afraid those old habits are deeply engrained."

John Mark had been studying the waters in front of the ship. Now he turned and even though he had not been part of the conversation, he offered, "Peter had a vision that said, 'Do not call anything impure that God has made clean'."

"Yes, that was clear," Paul said with impatience. "God made the bull clean, but some tanner made its skin stink. I know we must sleep under the shelter of hides. I simply do not care for the awful smell." He had heard enough quotes of Peter for the morning.

Three days later, their time of prayer and worship had introduced the discussion of preaching to the Gentiles. Barnabas said, "Granted, we will begin by meeting in the synagogues where there are many devout Jews. But we are a great distance from the temple and its reverence." Looking directly at John Mark, he asked, "Can you recall Peter's proclamation in the temple?"

John Mark could remember it clearly. "We call that the five points of preaching." He held up one finger, saying, "The age of fulfillment has dawned. A new order is being inaugurated, and the chosen are summoned to join in the new community." He held up his second finger, "This new age has come through the life, death and resurrection of Jesus Christ, all of which are in direct fulfillment of the prophecies of the scriptures. They are the result of the plan and foreknowledge of God." Finger number three reminded him to say, "By the virtue of the resurrection, Jesus has been exalted to the right hand of God and is head of the new Israel." Raising his fourth finger, John Mark said, "These events will soon reach their completion in the return of Christ in glory and judgment of the living and the dead." As he raised his thumb, he concluded, "These facts are made the grounds for an appeal for repentance. They offer forgiveness of sins, the gift of the Holy Spirit, and the promise of eternal life." John Mark's smile bloomed with satisfaction.

Paul studied that happy face for a moment, then replied, "I'm glad not to hear the condemning voice of Simon Peter telling how our forefathers abused the prophets and our own sinfulness finally executed Jesus. The people we will have the privilege of addressing have little awareness of Hebrew history and no interest in our politics. When we speak about guilt, there is more than enough to go around and a universal hunger for righteousness."

John Mark was about to reply, but Barnabas pressed his knee against the back of the lad, saying, "Your wisdom is evident, Paul. Speaking to these new believers is a great privilege. It is one we must always enter with much prayer."

"That is correct," the former Pharisee said softly. "As our young friend has pointed out, we are entering a new era of God's promises. I believe we can walk the narrow way with caution and preparation." Paul's eyes held those of John Mark's. After a silent moment both men looked away.

John Mark studied the distant shoreline. He pondered how it could be that someone as highly trained as a Pharisee could still be so unaware of his own errant behavior. Before he could finish that thought he was distracted by the voices of the sailors who said that they would be in the port of Seleucia before dark. Suddenly the prospect of new fellowships and preaching crowded out the distraction of the irritation of a travelling companion.

Dusk shadows had claimed the harbor of Seleucia by the time the ship was securely moored. Paul suggested that the expense of an inn would be welcome to him, but Barnabas thought their accommodations aboard would be more practical for one more night.

"We can have an early departure and be in Antioch by mid day. I'm sure there are many people who are eager for our arrival, and the continuation of our fellowship with them."

John Mark found the fragrance of leather pleasant for one more night.

The following days were a blur of happy reunion gatherings. It seemed that everywhere Barnabas and Paul went there were crowds of people to worship with them. They had a new name for their fellowship. Some called themselves "Christian," of the party of Christ. They began with sincere prayers of gratitude, followed by songs of faith. There were reports of significant growth and stories of spiritual wonder. More prayers for healing and strengthening followed, and finally an offering to help support the mission they were on. Eventually the brothers laid hands on the three, affirming that God was at work in them and sending them forth led by the Holy Spirit. Barnabas said he felt guided toward Cyprus, the place of his birth. They set sail for the port of Salamis.

It took them nearly three months to work their way across the island. Their routine was established to meet the people gathering in the synagogues. Barnabas would introduce the three and, like the Levite he was, would lead them in prayer and songs. Paul would remind them of the activity of God in the past to create a righteous community and Israel's inability to remain faithful to the covenant. He would conclude his account by introducing the life, death and resurrection of Jesus. Barnabas would give an impassioned invitation for people to repent and accept forgiveness of their sins. Then he would guide them into the knowledge of God's Holy Spirit, which was present and at work in each person there. Many believed, and those who could not quite accept the new concept wanted to hear more about it. John Mark quietly made notes on every gathering. His companions began shortening his name to Mark.

Elymas

When they reached Paphos, the western port, a most unusual thing happened. The proconsul, Sergius Paulus, an intelligent man, sent for them because he wanted to hear the word of God. An attendant of the proconsul named Elymas, however, decided to oppose them. Perhaps he wanted to protect his position or impress the proconsul. Elymas means 'wise man' or 'magician.' He continued to interrupt or challenge the validity of Paul's teaching. Finally, filled with the Holy Spirit, Paul looked straight at him and said, "You are a child of the devil and an enemy of all that is right! You are full of all kinds of deceit and trickery. Will you never stop perverting the right ways of the Lord? Now the hand of the Lord is against you. You are going to be blind, and for a time you will be unable to see the light of the sun."

Immediately mist and darkness came over Elymas, and he groped about, seeking someone to lead him by the hand. When the proconsul saw what happened, he believed, for he was amazed at the teaching about the Lord. The missionaries could have stayed much longer in Paphos as the retelling of that account spread through the city, but Paul was convinced in prayer that they were being called to Pamphylia. They found a ship bound for Perga.

Irreconcilable Differences

On the second morning of their journey, Paul was perusing the pages of notes Mark had written so far. He was impressed with both the style and content.

"Mark," he said with some surprise, "these are very good. You have been paying close attention to our work. Anyone can see these were written by an accomplished secretary." He was quiet as he read a bit more. "I owe you an apology. I underestimated your ability, allowing your youth to hide the accomplished craftsman. I am truly sorry for my oversight."

"Thank you," the young man said sincerely. "I recall that Peter asked Jesus how many times we should forgive others. He thought seven times would be gracious, but Jesus told him that seven times seventy times would be better. I believe we must be in continual forgiveness."

"And I believe I have heard all the quotes from Simon Peter that I can tolerate," the frustrated man retorted. He would have said more but an irritated Mark sprang to the defense.

"Even you must be aware of the hours I have spent writing Peter's recollections and wisdom over the past two years. I have spent more time with him than with my own father. Why would I not want to quote the man who has done more to shape my faith than any other?" He would have continued but now the debate turned personal, and unkind.

"Perhaps if you had spent more time with a teacher gaining a bit of education, you would have written something worth repeating," Paul said. There was a moment of silence as both men tried to control the tone of the conversation. Finally Paul continued, "Peter is a hypocrite. After his Joppa vision, he ate with Gentiles. But when the Jerusalem brothers came to Antioch, Peter was quick to eat only with the Jews. He fell back into his old way. I called his hypocrisy clearly before them all. He even confused Barnabas into avoiding the Gentiles, so do not quote him to me again."As Paul spoke his voice became more abrasive.

"You called the one whom Jesus identified as the 'rock upon which his church would be built' a hypocrite? You publicly insulted one who is an apostle?" There were tears in Mark's eyes, suddenly beyond forgiving this affront. "Once a Pharisee, always a Pharisee" Mark growled. "You are good at condemning and pointing out the failure of others. You persecuted the fellowship until your little fainting spell on the road to Damascus, but I do not believe your heart was changed. Like a puffed up rooster, you are still a Pharisee." He reached over and removed the pages from Paul's hand, returning them to his pouch. "You won't hear more quotes from me, nor will you need to put up with my company. Get yourself another assistant." It was just then that Barnabas came on deck.

"This seems to be an out-of-the-ordinary conversation between brothers who are sharing the good news," he said brightly. Paul silently stepped around him, heading for his bunk.

Mark said, "I offended Paul with one too many quotes from Peter. Is it true that he insulted Peter for eating with the Jewish delegation from Jerusalem?"

Now Barnabas understood that this conversation was heated and quite serious.

"Well, yes there was a bit of a dispute about whether we should eat with the Gentiles or respect the mood of those from Jerusalem who may not have been so comfortable with the idea. I think the only one who was upset about the whole matter was Paul. He wanted to be clear that old restrictions no longer applied." Concerned eyes searched Mark's face. "Tell me what I can do to ease this situation."

Mark shook his head saying, "I don't believe you can do anything. I am not willing to continue this effort with a man who is so full of bitterness and judgment. I know you need to stay with him, but I do not. I am sorry to leave you in this way, but I can find a ship headed for Caesarea. Father made sure I had adequate funds to return. I'm sure there is positive work to be done in the region of Decapolis. We will meet again when your trip is completed."

For a day and a half Paul stayed in his bunk, complaining of a slight but growing fever. Mark stayed on deck most of the time, avoiding further confrontation. Barnabas tried as best he could to comfort his mission mates. ★(Acts 13:13)

Home

Even at a distance, Silvanus could recognize the strong stride of his son.

"Mary," he called happily toward the house, "John Mark is home!" He hurried down the path to the road to greet him. After a strong embrace, he asked, "Are the others behind you?"

"No, I am alone. I found it very challenging to put up with the constant bitterness of Paul. He seems to have a deep aversion of Simon Peter. I finally had to make a choice, which was not that difficult. I'm glad to be home." The son's eyes held fast to his father's. Mary joined the happy welcoming hug.

Silvanus was eager to tell his son about the recent activity of the brothers in Jerusalem. "I just returned from delivering another support offering. James asked about the chronicle you have written about the years of Jesus' ministry. He tells me that the Apostle Matthew has gathered many of the lessons Jesus taught, the sayings that brought hope and life to many. James asked if you would mind if Matthew copies the scroll, adding that material that would be of special interest to Hebrew readers. Would you mind if your scroll might be used in that new way?" There was such enthusiasm in his voice that John Mark understood his father's appreciation and encouragement to continue the project.

"It was written to be read by as many as possible," John Mark said brightly. "To have the addition of another apostle's memories would make it only that much more precious. When do they want it delivered?"

A stern expression changed his father's face as he answered, "The atmosphere is changing in Jerusalem. No longer may the brothers teach in the temple without sharp resistance. Since the death of John's brother, there has been more and more angry opposition from the Jews. I believe our days in Jerusalem are numbered. Perhaps we should invite Matthew to do his work here in the tranquility of the vineyard."

"Perhaps our opposition is not only in Jerusalem," his son replied. Then he shared the episode with Elymas, and Paul's powerful defense. "The magician was still staggering about, led around by someone's hand when we left. These seem like drastic days to me."

Silvanus nodded saying, "The word James used was 'crucial.' The future is truly in the balance. Our courage and commitment will be tested. He said there is tremendous opportunity to spread the words of Jesus. I'm so glad you are home." Another hardy hug emphasized the truth of his words. "If you are rested, we can leave in the morning for Jerusalem. I'm sure James will want to hear about your work in Cyprus and the good work Barnabas and Paul are doing."

Dawn was chasing the shadows of darkness when they set out at a brisk pace. John Mark carried a travelling bag and a leather cylinder which safely held the scroll with two years of careful effort. Just before mid-day they caught up with a caravan of merchants. Silvanus suggested they slow their pace a bit to take advantage of the security in such a large group that was obviously on their way to Jerusalem. His son questioned whether it was security or the easier pace his father was after. All in all, the trip promised to be satisfying.

James the Leader

Following the caravan must have been more efficient because it was still morning on the third day when they made their way to the modest house in the Jewish district. John Mark thrilled at the greeting they received from Simon Peter, and then he was surprised at the obvious status his father enjoyed in the fellowship. James introduced himself to John Mark and listened intently to his report of the work done in Antioch and then Cyprus. The leader smiled as the young man tried to soften the disagreement with Paul.

"I tried to forget that he was the Pharisee that persecuted the believers here; but when he openly insulted Simon Peter, I knew I could not support such divergent loyalties," he said a bit embarrassed.

"Loyalty is a fragile flower," James said softly, "and its division most harmful." Perhaps he was thinking about how he himself had at first questioned his older brother's vision and offered no loyalty. "You have proven your ability to be an ambassador of the gospel. There is more than a little need for the word to be spread. At times the task seems monumental. You will become a strong voice for spreading the word." Then brightening and changing the subject to the more urgent matter of the scroll, he said, "Silvanus has invited Matthew to work on another scroll in the quiet of the vineyard, using your marvelous work as a guide. Thomas has agreed to come along if there are still some towns who have not heard about Jesus. Perhaps Gadara may become a haven for apostles who are looking to the northern cities."

Matthew had been studying the scroll. He looked at John Mark with admiration, saying, "It is masterful! I can hear the very voice of Simon Peter in this work. You have created a document for the ages."

John Mark was embarrassed by the praise, especially after the words of James. Humbly he said, "It's not quite finished. I simply wrote what I heard them saying. The praise is not for me but for them, and to the Lord God who has appeared to us and empowered us to witness to his glory."

Matthew nodded in agreement. "We must always be aware of God's praise," he said softly. "If I can make the addition of information that might be of interest to Hebrew readers, showing the prophecies fulfilled and some of the other teachings and sayings of Jesus, I believe it will serve a new audience. I believe Andrew recalls some other teachings of Jesus as well. Perhaps the same thing might happen for the Greek readers, if an even wider selection of miracles might be included and the wonder of Jesus' efforts to include all people, there is no limit. Each of us has a particular point of view and ability that can add to the blessings." All the men who were in the house gathered around to inspect the scroll.

James finally said, "I believe we are in the presence of the Holy Spirit who will use these men and their ability to continue the work that has just begun. Let us worship together in prayer and bless these scrolls, for they will march into times and places after we are gone." Fervent prayers filled the room.

Yet Another Confirmation Class

The confirmation class had not even started when Jenny raised her hand and began to ask her question before Pastor Randle could recognize her. "Pastor, are you going to tell us about spiritual presents today?" There was an immature exuberance in her voice.

"If you mean 'spiritual gifts,' yes, that's our confirmation topic today."

Once again his confirmand added, "Yes, that's it. Mom and I were talking about that last night. She said I should listen carefully so I can tell her about it later. She sounded very interested. Do we get to request our gifts like making a wish list?"

The pastor chuckled and said, "No, these are skills that God gives to make the church strong and effective. I'm glad to know that you can be a student and a teacher too. Look at the list I've handed out. Do you see that 1Corinthians 12 is the chapter we are assigned to read? The main subject for this part of the epistle is the essential unity of the church. I've printed it for you so we can read it together."

He waited until he knew they were all ready, then he began: *"There are distinctions between different kinds of special gifts, but there is one and the same Spirit. There are distinctions between different kinds of service, but there is one and the same Lord. There are distinctions between different kinds of effects, but it is one and the same God who causes them all in every person. To each there is given a unique mixture of manifestations of the Spirit, and always toward some beneficial end. To one person there is given through the Spirit the word of wisdom; to another the word of knowledge, by the same Spirit; to still another faith, by the same Spirit; to another, the special gifts of healing through the one and the same Spirit; to another, the ability to produce wonderful deeds of power; to another prophecy; to another the ability to distinguish between different kinds of spirits; to another different kinds of tongues; to another the power to interpret tongues. One and the same Spirit produces all these effects, sharing them out individually to each person as He wishes."*

Pastor Randle smiled warmly and said, "I don't expect you to fully understand all that we are studying today. This is a subject that you may dwell on for years. Just know that God has gifts to empower the church to fulfill its ministry to the world. I have made a list of the most familiar ones, and again I want to emphasize that the purpose of these gifts is to build up the ministry of the church in unity." He held up a sheet of paper that had been distributed to them.

"The first ones that Paul mentioned are 'knowledge and wisdom.' It seems like those are pretty much the same, but knowledge relates to our understanding of the divine nature and timeless truth of God. It is a gift given so we can understand the marvelous care and compassion our righteous God has for us. Wisdom is the application or practical use that Holy Nature might have for us and others through Christ, for justice and peace in the world.

"Paul goes on to mention faith, which is the ability to extend one's basic belief to serve corporate and individual needs specifically related to the life and ministry of the church, the body of Christ. Faith is the confidence that pushes fear aside. Then he identifies healing, which is the ability to cure or be cured of illness that might hinder effective ministries for Christ, the church or individuals. When Paul speaks of wonderful deeds of power he is referring to the ability to do powerful works that transcend our perception of natural laws and means to free the church or individuals from conditions that restrict needed ministries.

"Then there are gifts for communication. Prophecy is not forecasting the future, but the ability to link biblical truths and God's will for today's living; it's a way of conveying God's righteousness and just living in today's world. We might substitute the word 'preaching' for it. The ability to distinguish between different kinds of spirits simply means telling the difference between good and evil, right and wrong, and what is of God, human nature or evil, and to use that knowledge for the protection and health of the body of Christ.

"Speaking in tongues is the ability to pray or praise God with beneficial wordless phrases or utterances not familiar as a known language. It is speaking or silence with such joy-filled intimacy with Christ that faith is strengthened and ministries become more effective. Then the interpretation of tongues is the ability to hear, comprehend and translate spiritual messages given by others so the larger body can understand. These two frequently go together.

"The rest of that printed page is a list of spiritual gifts that are identified elsewhere in scripture by Paul: teaching, which is the ability to discern, analyze, and deliver biblical and other spiritual truths to help others accept and understand the clear calling of God to live justly and righteously.

"Exhortation is the ability to encourage, motivate, inspire and strengthen others to live out God's will and calling. It's the cheerfulness gift.

"Generosity is the ability to manage one's resources of income, time and energy to exceed what is considered to be a reasonable standard of giving to the church, an amount that brings joy and power to do more for further service.

"Mercy is the ability to identify with and actually feel the physical, mental, spiritual, or emotional pain of others and feeling the necessity to do something to relieve them."

"Hospitality," he continued the list, "is more than just throwing a good party. It is the ability to extend caring and sharing to others beyond your close friends to demonstrate the unlimited and inclusive companionship of Christ.

"Leadership, which I personally believe to be a necessity to be a pastor, is the ability to envision God's will and purpose for the church and to demonstrate compelling skills in capturing the imaginations, energies, and skills of others to pursue and accomplish God's will.

"Administration is one of my favorite Greek words. It means the work of a ship's pilot who steers around the rocks and shoals to a safe harbor. They are the people who have the ability to organize and implement church ministries with eventful results.

"Scripture identifies at least two dozen or more spiritual gifts, all of which are for the efficiency and harmony of church unity. There is even one that I think you would especially appreciate, Danny. It is humor, the ability to bring laughter and joy to situations to relieve tension, anxiety or conflicts and to free emotions and energies needed for effective ministries." He traded grins with the student. "But in the end Paul goes on to say that there is a gift greater than all the others. The danger always is that those who have different gifts will differ with each other. That sort of spirit can only hinder the church's effective ministry. There is only one thing that can bind the church into a perfect unity, and that is love, which is the ability to see others as the Lord God sees them, precious in every way. Your homework for this week is to read the 13th chapter of 1 Corinthians not just once or twice, but ten times."

There was general groaning because the assignment sounded difficult. But when Pastor Randle uncovered the tray of Crispy Cream doughnuts, they all knew the class was finishing on a positive note.

The Attraction of the
Missionary Road

When it was time to return to Gadara, James prayed for their effective witness and their safety. During the brief visit, a great deal of enthusiasm had been generated for more than Matthew's scroll. When Thomas said he wanted to be a part of the next mission, Andrew, the brother of Simon Peter, said he did too. Simon, sometimes called the Zealot, expressed his desire to help with the scroll. He assured them that he could recall most clearly the lessons Jesus had taught them. There were still visible stars as the six passed through the gate headed north. This time there was no caravan to set the pace, but John Mark was pretty sure they were walking more briskly.

By evening they were resting on a hill overlooking the well at Sychar. Andrew was reminiscing about the conversation Jesus had there with the woman who had a complicated marital history. ★(John 4:7ff) "He spoke with her patiently, even when she would bring up some diversion. Jesus had a way of helping people at the core of their problems." Andrew was quiet for a moment before asking, "Do you remember that she was so eager to go back into the town that had snubbed her that she left her water jug?" He chuckled, "She was so eager to tell them about our Jesus who had brought her forgiveness and purpose. I wonder how they are getting along these days."

Silvanus asked, "Would you like to spend a few days in Sychar? I'd be happy to accompany you and find out how you go about establishing contact with the people."

With a broad smile Andrew answered, "I would welcome your company. But I have been thinking about names. Your name is Silas in the Hebrew form. Would you mind if we use it instead?" Then as though he had been wondering about John Mark, he added, "And you, our young scholar, should just be Mark. It would be a name unique to our group, which would help some of us slow fishermen." His laughter was rich enough to make them all smile. There was no more conversation about names, so the planning of a mission up the west side of the Sea of Galilee took them into darkness. Four would continue to Gadara and two would join them there later.

The first two days back in the vineyard, Mark was busy establishing a work table where Matthew could spread out his notes and scroll. Mark also had to listen to a concerned disciple who wanted him to finally finish his marvelous work. "You were present when the risen Lord appeared to us," Matthew said in wonder. "Simply relate that account and your scroll will be complete."

"You are right, of course," Mark replied apologetically. "Thomas and I have been talking about the towns to the east, Gerasa, Capitolas, Arbela and Pella. In the time it would take me to finish the scroll we could introduce the Lord to many new worshipers. I can always get back to it later." Matthew tried to stress the importance the written account would be to the future. Mark's only answer was the urgent need to spread the word in this present day.

The night before they were to leave, Mark talked with his mother about their plans.

"It sounds like a very large undertaking," she said softly. "Do you actually believe you can visit six cities?" She studied the eyes she had loved since infancy.

"They are not very distant, so I'm sure we can visit them. If you are asking can we help form a fellowship of believers in each one, I can only say we will try."

"Then will you promise to be back by the Festival of Booths? The grapes will be picked and resting in the aging vats." Her tender eyes searched his for assurance

"Once again mother," his voice was tender, "I can tell you that we will try. If we have great success there may be some that ask us to stay longer. That would also be a productive dream."

Mary placed her hand on Mark's cheek. "Your father loves us very much and has become accustomed to the warmth of our small family, as I have as well. I know that he wants us to celebrate as many festivals as possible together. Now he hopes to make up for the many that he missed. He traded his time for a financially worry-free life for us and the ability to give generously to those in need, which he has done faithfully." She was still, but not satisfied with her answer. "He sees his role as provider to keep us safe and secure."

"It seems that he has found a way to share love with a wide range of people," Mark whispered. "He has given me a model of God's embracing care."

"One day you will own this vineyard and will take a wife to yourself and have children. Then you will see how complete your father's love has been for all of us." She tenderly embraced her son, not knowing it was for the last time.

Wanting to quiet his mother's dread, the son said, "I will never be further from home than a couple days' walk. There is no reason to miss the Festival of Booths." A gentle kiss on her cheek sealed the promise.

All the way to Gerasa Thomas and Mark talked about their strategy and assignments. Mark was glad that Thomas had something of a plan based on his success in the past. Mark was also sure that the expectations for his contribution were well within his capabilities. There were three synagogues in Gerasa, so they would visit the first one on Sabbath eve and a second one in the morning. Then they could make decisions about the length of their stay.

The two guests stood in the back as the opening prayers were said and Sabbath Psalters sung. They listened to the reading from the law and then from the prophet Isaiah. The moderator asked if there were any guests who would like to share their understanding from the lessons or bring news from outside, which was the invitation Thomas was waiting to hear.

He raised his hand, and when recognized said, "Thank you for the gracious welcome we have received this evening. I am Thomas of Jerusalem. My Greek friends call me Didymus, the twin. Can you imagine two such handsome specimens?" The gathering chuckled at his humor for in fact handsome is not a word that would describe his appearance. "My father was an officer in the Roman army and my mother a Hebrew that made sure I was properly raised. It is not an unfamiliar story." There was more chuckling amusement at his comment. "My brother has followed my father's leadership, and I am here to tell you about the most unusual occurrence in Jerusalem the week before Passover. Perhaps you heard about it. It began when a rabbi from Nazareth approached the city riding on a young donkey. Yes, that could be understood as a visiting king coming in peace. Many pilgrims were quick to pick up the significance and lined the road calling out 'Hosanna! Blessed is he who comes in the name of the Lord! Hosanna!'"

Thomas went on in a more confidential voice, "As soon as he entered the Temple he went straight to the money changer's tables, over-turning them and opening the cages. He said loudly, 'God's house shall be a place of prayer, not a den for robbers.' That was too much for the Pharisees and Sadducees. Just before the Sabbath they had him arrested, whipped, and with a questionable trial, sentenced to be crucified along with two robbers.

"I'm telling you this because I was one of his students. He had predicted his death and promised to rise from the grave on the third day." Now heads were shaking in disbelief. "I know how you are feeling. I said the same thing. 'I'll believe it if I place my finger in the nail print in the palm of his hand or place my hand where the spear entered his side' were my exact words. Friends, on the third day he came into the place where we were staying. He promised us that he would be with us always in risen power. Then he offered me his hands to touch, his wounded side. I could only answer, 'My Lord and my God.'"

It was obvious to all that Thomas was becoming emotional about the things he was saying. Finally he said, "This young man is Mark from Gadara. He is a winemaker and scribe, writing an account of these wondrous things. Let me ask him to tell you just one of the rabbi's memorable teachings." The crowd shifted their attention to the tall lad who was rather handsome.

"Thank you for your attention," he began. "We know there was a time when the world was dark and without form; *but God* (he emphasized the words) said 'Let there be light, and it was so. There was a time when we were not a people; *but God* said to Abraham, 'Your descendents will be like the sand of the shore' and it was so. There was a time when Israel was enslaved in Egypt; *but God* told Moses to cry out, 'Let my people go!' And it was so. This may very well be a time for some who are here today who feel separated from God, lost, angry, hopeless, filled with guilt; *but God* has sent us to say that whoever believes in God's loving mercy and will confess their sin, they will be forgiven and filled with God's Holy Spirit. If you walked in here as a sinner, there is no need to walk out the same way. God wants to forgive you, and it will be so.

"Jesus once told the story of two men who went into the temple to pray, one was a Pharisee, and the other was a tax collector. The Pharisee stood up and prayed about himself: 'God, I thank you that I am not like other men – robbers, evil-doers, adulterers – or even like this tax collector. I fast twice a week and give a tithe of all I get.'

"But the tax collector stood at a distance. He would not even look up to heaven, but beat his breast and said, 'God, have mercy on me a sinner.'"

Mark's voice was intimate as he quietly told them, "Jesus said, 'I tell you that this man, rather than the other went home justified before God. For everyone who exalts himself will be humbled, and he who humbles himself will be exalted.'" The room was silent with several drying the tears from their face.

Another song was shared and a lengthy prayer by the moderator, then a Sabbath blessing. As people were making their way out, several wanted to talk with Thomas and Mark. There was an eagerness to keep them in Gerasa. They were given directions to the second synagogue, and more important, to the oval forum just up the hill where a wider audience could hear them. Thomas agreed to greet whoever might be interested tomorrow after the ninth hour. There was so much more about Jesus that he wanted to share with them. A man with a roof terrace offered its use and meal hospitalities if they could remain for a week. Thomas had a wide smile as he agreed.

That scenario repeated itself again and again in the following cities. They were in Gerasa seven weeks. By the time they had finished their tour of the other five cities, they were thrilled to know that strong fellowships had been established in each place. Mark, however, had missed the Festival of Booths. He urged Thomas to return to Gadara with him.

House of Sorrow

When they finally turned into the lane from the road they had been on since early dawn, Mark sensed there was something wrong. There were no lamps lit in the twilight shadows of the house, nor were there any voices to be heard. He was still some distance from it when he called a greeting for his mother. The house remained nonresponsive. Just as Mark was about to open the door, Johanan came from the winepress, calling a greeting to his young friend. By his slumped posture Mark knew the news he was about to hear was not welcome.

"Mr. Mark, sir, it is so good to see your return. By the darkness of your house, you must have understood that something very sad has occurred." He paused, choosing his words carefully. "Shortly after you left, your mother developed a fever, which became very serious. Several of the women from the fellowship tried to comfort her." The man's gaze turned toward the ground. "But she did not survive," he said softly. "Without Mr. Silvanus or you to give direction, we felt it necessary to prepare her for burial nearby. Mr. Silvanus returned with another man about a month ago. He attended to all the expenses of her burial. About a week after he returned Mr. Barnabas and another man also returned from a long journey. They brought a gift offering for the men in Jerusalem, so everyone left together. They asked me to tell you to join them there, if you will, sir." It was obvious that the one who welcomed instructions was uncomfortable giving them.

At first light the following morning with little rest and only a drachma in their travelling bags, Mark and Thomas set out for Jerusalem. Their pace was too brisk for conversation, but Thomas attempted to ease the sense of guilt Mark was feeling for being unavailable to assist his mother when she so needed him.

"You had no way of knowing that she would become ill," he said between deep breaths. "There was nothing you could have given her more than the good women who tried to relieve her illness." Finally he said, "You call others to repentance, assuring them of God's forgiveness. You have confessed your absence, now receive holy forgiveness." Finally, Thomas said softly, "God has already forgiven you." They hurried on.

Thomas was guiding their path through the twists and turns of the Jewish District when approaching them through the crowd Mark recognized his father and Barnabas. He called for their attention and then knelt before his father. The words tumbled out, "I am so sorry I was not there to help mother. I had no idea she was so sick. I should have…"

His father interrupted the passionate speech by helping his son stand and gave him a warm embrace. "Son, there was nothing any of us could have done," the father comforted. "I'm sure Mary would have welcomed our presence if she could have been aware. But she was very ill." Then speaking very softly he added, "Do not confuse your grief with guilt. We are both wishing we had been there." Barnabas joined the embrace also expressing joy in seeing his nephew and Thomas.

The apostle echoed their happy welcome, admitting that the travelers had not eaten so far this day.

It only took a few days of reports and worship of praise for the crowd to realize the limitations of the cramped rooms. They were each eager to be back to the task of witnessing. The mission trails were beckoning to them. Perhaps Paul was the most vocal. He was convinced Macedonia and Achaia was a prime region, with Athens, the seat of intellect, and Corinth, the bed of sin. Barnabas offered to accompany him, and to their surprise so did Mark.

The smile that had bloomed on Paul's face at the offer of Barnabas now faded into a scowl and he said, "I have little confidence in someone who is so undependable. I must decline your offer, Mark. Luke, the physician from Macedonia, has proven a competent secretary.

He is already finishing a copy of your first incomplete draft, and plans to add the recollections of Andrew, as well as a more current second scroll." The room was suddenly still with such an immediate rejection. ★(Acts 15:39)

Barnabas said quietly, "Paul, you may want to reconsider all the good work Mark and Thomas have accomplished. He is more mature now and polished."

"It is not necessary for me to reconsider. He is a quitter whom I cannot trust." He did not raise his voice but there was a dreadful silence around Paul.

"But I do trust him," Barnabas replied. "I believe God's wonderful Spirit has been poured into him and the fellowships will be powerfully blessed. I will reconsider and go with Mark to Cyprus, and then we will follow God's guidance." There were whispered responses, but no one spoke out.

"Paul, if you need a companion, I'll go with you," Silvanus, now known as Silas, said quietly. "I know the region well and have many contacts that might be favorable to you." He gave a tender nod toward Mark to affirm the decisions that were being made. Three days later, after considerable prayer and encouragement, the apostles went their mission ways. Fortunately there was an opportunity for Silas to speak privately with his son.

After expressing his joy in Mark's stature and accomplishments, his father embraced him tenderly. "We may not see one another for a season or two. I hope we can always meet here in Jerusalem. We will be too busy to continue to own the vineyard. I will take care of that. As you go north, however, take from the vineyard whatever you need for your journey. I want you to look in the pitcher for night water in your room." The son smiled, delighted in the notion that the seldom used vessel might hold a secret. "You will find a small pouch with enough gold coins to help you travel back to Cyprus and provide you plenty of nourishment." He did not release his embrace for there was more to share. "If you are in the region of Miletus and in need of assistance, go to the Innkeeper named Luscious above the Didyma harbor. He is an employee of mine and is keeping an account for you as well. He manages several properties I came to own while serving the governor. When he asks for proof, make a sigma crossed by another sigma. He will recognize my symbol." Silas took in a large breath, "John Mark, it is also possible that we may not see one another again. If that should be the case I want you to know that I have always been so very proud of you. You are a perfect son. My love might not have been well expressed, but you have always warmed my heart." They were words that warmed the son's as well.

A Bold Mission Journey

An excited Mark was explaining the opportunity to his uncle. "I know we agreed to return to Cyprus, but that is not expanding the introduction of Jesus, it is merely revisiting last year's work. There is available passage on a coastal freighter carrying supplies to the Roman forces in the north. They are stopping in Miletus and then Sparta. Think of it! None of the brothers have journeyed so far north. We could introduce Jesus to cities that have never had a chance to accept him." His youthful smile made Barnabas glad they were taking this journey together.

"But, Mark, we know no one who might introduce us there. There is no supporting fellowship, only the established synagogues," the cautious uncle replied. "You are talking about a challenge which only a seasoned witness could attempt."

"Exactly my point," the lad countered. "There will be others who come after us who will find the fruit of our labor in growing fellowships along the way." He paused then revealed his best argument. "Besides, my father has told me that a man in Didyma is holding an account for me that will guarantee our return, whatever our success visiting the new cities."

"In this world," Barnabas said with a grin, "there are very few guarantees. It would be my pleasure to see one for myself. When does the ship leave?"

Two weeks later they were on the hillside above the Didyma port, seeking directions to the inn. What they found was a plain but clean building with no identifying sign. Knocking on the door, Mark said to the innkeeper that answered, "Good day, sir. I am John, son of Silvanus of Cyprus. I believe you are holding our account."

The man raised his eyebrows saying with only a little humor, "Ho, there are men who come here claiming to be my long lost half-brother and promising to pay me lavishly later for hospitality today. What proof do you have that what you are saying is true?"

Mark bent down and using his finger made the sigma sign in the dust; then turning to the side, he made another crossing on top of it. "I think it looks like a four petal flower."

From behind him, Barnabas said, "Or a cross with rounded arms, that certain Pharisees might find objectionable." With his foot he wiped the image back into the dust.

The expression on the innkeeper's face became gracious. "Please come in Mr. John. I hope I get to see your father soon. It has been quite a while since he was with us." He led them into a pleasant dining room with only six tables, all of which were empty. "May I get you a tray of figs and cheese? Perhaps some cool wine?"

"Thank you, Luscious. It is our plan to go on to Miletus yet today. I only wanted to introduce myself and my Uncle Barnabas, from Cyprus also."

The innkeeper hurried away, only to quickly return with a filled tray of figs, boiled fish and bread. Two glasses of wine mixed with water promised the thirsty men refreshment. He pulled up a chair and quietly told them this account: "Several years ago I was struggling to make this inn a profitable business. When the tax time came I was on the ragged edge, two years behind on my taxes, when the Romans decided to eat and drink me bare. They cleaned me out, then destroyed the place when I had nothing more to offer. I couldn't pay my tax for the third year. I and my family were marked to be sold as slaves and the inn confiscated."

He shook his head in remembrance of the awful time.

"Your father paid the taxes for me, and satisfied the back debts. He discovered who the soldiers were that did all the damage and had them compensate him for the destruction. He then had them sent to the northern front. The word was circulated that this inn was now the possession of the governor and any destruction would be severely punished. We have had a decade of tranquility. My son is the navigator for ships, my oldest daughter is married to a weaver of linens, and my youngest is betrothed. This inn belongs to your father, but he has given me the privilege of being blessed by its profits. I also manage several other properties that he owns in the region, collecting rent and taxes from them, for which I am also generously compensated." He opened a scroll and reported, "The balance of your account, sir, is twenty eight thousand drachma."

Both Barnabas and Mark were in stunned silence by the report.

"Your father has been our savior." His chin quivered and his voice broke.

A bit later when Mark offered to pay for their food, the innkeeper was quick to say that it had been an honor to meet the son of Silvanus. "There will always be a grateful table for you here," the happy man said.

A Surprising Outcome After Failure

By evening the travelers were on the outskirts of Miletus. It was too late to find a synagogue, so they chose an olive grove to rest until the Sabbath morning. As they chatted into the dusk, Barnabas asked if Mark had given any thought to the possible use of his surprise bounty.

"When I heard the report there was a moment of surprise. I am continually realizing the complexity of my own father. There is so much about him that was never shared. But honestly, I have only imagined how much good that account could accomplish in a fellowship, how many needy people could be blessed." The young man smiled as he thought about it.

Barnabas shared a quiet compliment, "Obviously Silas anticipated the possibility of your future need. I'm proud that you didn't fall into a mire of seduction. Your spirit continues to show its maturity and the correctness of our choice to be this far from Jerusalem." They talked into the gathering evening about their introduction to a congregational gathering in the morning and the roles they would take.

The synagogue turned out to be less than they expected. The room was quite spacious, but the attendance was sparse. Mark said, "Perhaps the main attendance was last evening." There were just over a dozen men there. Finally after the cantor sang a familiar song, the moderator read a selection from the Law and then a portion of the Prophet Isaiah. A lengthy prayer was followed by a lack-luster welcome to any visitors and the invitation to comment on the selected readings. Barnabas raised his hand to speak.

He explained the history of the people of God who tried but failed to keep the covenant and that God sent prophets and priests to try to restore the brokenness. "The prophet is speaking about

God's ultimate attempt to reach the people who had failed again. 'Surely he took up our infirmities and carried our sorrows, yet we considered him stricken by God, smitten by him and afflicted. But he was pierced for our transgressions, he was crushed for our iniquities, the punishment that brought us peace was upon him, and by his wounds we are healed. We all, like sheep have gone astray, each of us have turned to our own way; and the Lord has laid upon him the iniquity of us all.' In the ultimate sacrifice, God took on a human form to relate to his people. For three years we have followed a teacher who is the very embodiment of his lessons. He performed powerful miracles, healed sickness and the lame. Some began calling him, 'Son of God.' The powerful Jewish leaders had him arrested, beaten, and crucified, all of which he had forecast. He also said that on the third day he would rise and we would see him again. Friends, I was in the room when that happened. He even showed us the terrible wounds."

Two men at the back left the room.

"My young friend has one of the teaching lessons Jesus gave us. This is Mark of Gadara, a winemaker and scribe who has recorded the events of Jesus." Barnabas sat down feeling that he had not won the attention of the small crowd.

"Good Sabbath," Mark said politely. "Jesus told his disciples, 'There was a man who had two sons. The younger one said to his father, 'Father, give me my share of the estate'" A couple listeners groaned in disbelief. "'So he divided his property between them.'

"'Not long after that, the younger son got together all he had, set off for a distant country, and there squandered his wealth in wild living. After he had spent everything, there was a severe famine in that whole country, and he began to be in need. So he went and hired himself out to a citizen of that country, who sent him to his field to feed pigs.'" There was more groaning at the notion. "'He longed to fill his stomach with the pods the pigs were eating, but no one gave him anything.'

107

"'When he came to his senses, he said, 'How many of my father's hired men have food to spare, and here I am starving to death! I will set out and go back to my father and say to him, 'Father I have sinned against heaven and against you. I am no longer worthy to be called your son; make me like one of your hired men.' So he got up and went to his father.'

"'But while he was still a long way off, his father saw him and was filled with compassion for him; he ran to his son, threw his arms around him and kissed him.'"

A voice from the back said, "No! He wouldn't do that!"

Mark continued the story. "'The son said to him, 'Father, I have sinned against heaven and against you. I am no longer worthy to be called your son.'

"'But the father said to his servants, 'Quick! Bring the best robe and put it on him. Put a ring on his finger and sandals on his feet. Bring the fatted calf and kill it. Let's have a feast and celebrate. For this son of mine was dead and is alive again; he was lost and is found.' So they began to celebrate.'

"'Meanwhile the older son was in the field. When he came near the house, he heard music and dancing. So he called one of the servants and asked him what was going on. 'Your brother has come,' he replied, and your father has killed the fatted calf because he has him back safe and sound.'

"'The older brother became angry and refused to go in. So his father came out and pleaded with him. But he answered his father, 'Look! All these years I've been slaving for you and never disobeyed your orders. Yet you never gave me even a young goat so I could celebrate with my friends. But when this son of yours who has squandered your property with prostitutes comes home, you kill the fatted calf for him!'

"'My son,' the father said, 'you are always with me, and everything I have is yours. But we have to celebrate and be glad, because this brother of yours was dead and is alive again; he was lost and is found.'"

Mark was silent for a long moment, then he continued, "The story is unfinished. You will probably think on its meaning several times today. Perhaps you will see yourself in the younger brother, making foolish decisions and wondering how you can ever be forgiven. Or perhaps you see yourself in the righteous angry older brother who resents the compassionate forgiveness that welcomes the sinner back into God's mercy. I can only tell you that the psalmist was not mistaken. God can create in you a clean heart today, and renew a right spirit within you."

A man wearing a scowl interrupted, "I heard that you are against the government and telling people to oppose it. Is that true?" There was no mistaking his disgust.

Mark said with a shocked voice, "No, that is definitely not the case. In fact, one day a troublemaker asked Jesus if it was right to pay taxes. Jesus asked the man to show him a coin. When the man produced one, the Master asked, 'Whose image does it bear?' The man said 'Caesar's.' Then Jesus said, 'Render unto Caesar that which is Caesar's and render unto God that which is God's.'"

When there were no other questions he sat down and the moderator concluded the worship with a brief prayer and no words of appreciation for the guests. The men all filed out silently.

The Call of Ephesus

All that is, except one, who waited by the door with a warm smile. Finally when they approached him, he embraced Barnabas like a brother, and then Mark.

"You were both outstanding! I know you have much to share. I'm only sorry for the dead ears of these men. I do believe they are from the Roman garrison stationed here. By the way I am Aquila of Ephesus now. We were from Rome originally, until Claudius Caesar's edict expelled us all from the city. I'm a tent maker here on a buying trip. Yesterday was a good day for me; on the docks I obtained enough hides to keep us busy for months." His smile broadened. "And today I meet two fascinating men who have opened a new avenue of thinking about God. Will you come to Ephesus sometime soon? We have a congregation that meets in our home. It's not large, but considerably more gracious than this one. We have heard about Jesus of Nazareth and are eager to hear more. I am also eager for you to meet my wife, who is the thinker in the family. She is the granddaughter of a rabbi who did the unthinkable. He carefully tutored her in religious thought. She must be careful when she talks to a rabbi, not to reveal the depth of her understanding." His effervescence was contagious. If the two missionaries hadn't considered a visit to Ephesus before, they surely were now.

Aquila sweetened the invitation by saying, "We have three wagonloads of hides. The one at the back is the largest, with a bench that can comfortably meet the needs of three of us. You are welcome to ride with me. We'll leave at dawn and be in Ephesus by dark, God willing."

Barnabas and Mark hardly had to consider the offer. God was once again providing an opportunity that would lead to more converts and deeper faith.

The pace of the oxen was methodical, yet still more speedy than a man could practically walk. The heavy wagon was a comfortable ride and their host was full of information. Mark was feeling like a very lucky traveler this morning.

Aquila was expounding on the city, saying "Ephesus is the capital city in the Roman province of Asia. There is a population of a quarter million people, comparable to Jerusalem during Passover. It is strategically located at the mouth of the Cayster River and is a significant center of commerce and banking. There are numerous temples, and the principal difference you will immediately see is that those temples are not devoted to Jehovah, but Greek gods, goddesses and emperors. Legend has it that the famous female Amazon women founded it; they set a stone statue of their mother goddess named Artemis Ephesia and established an annual circular dance, complete with scantily clad women carrying shields with swords and spears." He chuckled and added, "No part of that seems interesting to me. The Temple of Artemis was built about 700 years ago. It is four times as large as the Parthenon and designated as a place of asylum or refuge.

"The Persians conquered the land about a hundred years later; and then Alexander the Great took charge about 300 years ago. One of his successor generals named Lysimachus built the enormous six mile wall around the city. Ephesus was under Greek rule until Attalus III bequeathed it to the Romans. That's when it replaced Pergamum as the capital of the province.

"I'm telling you all of this history to help you understand our complicated worship scene. The Temple of Artemis is still major in the hearts of many of our citizens. It has hundreds of prostitute priestesses who ply the city nightly. There was an altar created in devotion to Augustus. It has changed through the years to become the site of emperor worship. Claudius seems to place little importance on it, but Caligula seemed to believe that he deserved it and more. In this city Caesar worship is quite significant, as you just witnessed, because there are so many Roman soldiers. You see, in Jerusalem you had one temple devoted to the One God. Any other worship was seen as idolatry, and the punishment was severe. In Ephesus, before you can convince your listeners of the goodness of the Lord God, you must win their hearts away from some other altar, and there are many."

Mark realized that their host was informing them that they had not only travelled a great distance from their home, they were also separated from a familiar way of life. The rhythm of the plodding oxen was a melody that carried them through the day.

The setting sun was finally releasing its warm grasp on the evening as the wagons stopped in front of a compound on the east side of the wall. They could see three large buildings in the shadows.

Aquila explained, "We could only afford to locate outside the city wall. This is something of a market area, but it is secure and very manageable. There's the house," he pointed to a building with a terrace on top. Nearby his hand directed them to another. "That one is where the hides are warehoused and tents are put together. The low one is the oxen shed. On warm afternoons they like nothing more than lying against the coolness of the city wall."

The driver of the front wagon had opened a gate while a woman ran toward them in greeting.

She wore no covering on her head so her hair flowed freely as she hurried to Aquila's side. Her tunic was shorter than most, so Mark could see that she wore no sandals, but her dazzling smile made everything else wane insignificantly.

"I am so happy to see you," she bubbled. "I have missed you terribly." Then she noticed the two others seated beside her husband. "And you have found travelling companions!" Her voice was rich and pleasant. All three men were returning her joy without saying a word. "I'll bet they are missionaries," she concluded her greeting, waiting for Aquila to introduce them.

"I have only been gone four days," he said happily.

"It seems twice that long to me. Who are your friends?" If he wasn't mindful of the courtesy, she would prod him.

"I visited the little morning synagogue again. This is Barnabas and Mark from Jerusalem." His voice emphasized the importance of the sacred city. "They spoke with such clarity and interest that I knew you would want to hear them. I think I interrupted their travel plans by offering a ride on the wagon. Or perhaps I impressed them with the promise that our fellowship would welcome them more warmly."

The men had climbed down from the wagon bench.

Her radiant smile did not diminish as she said, "He was too excited to tell you that I am Prisca, or Priscilla if you really want my attention." She held out her hands to clasp theirs. They had no idea of the depth or breadth of the relationship they were beginning.

"Come inside," she said brightly. "I have a tray of food for you, since I am pretty sure that the wagon's hospitality was sparse." There were tiny wrinkles at the corner of her eyes when she smiled with humor.

Aquila said, "Gentlemen, you may choose where you sleep tonight. The terrace is spacious and available, as is the display tent, which has three sections, with comfortable mats in two of them."

Barnabas asked, "Where will we be out of the way?"

Their host responded immediately, "You will have more privacy in the tent. The terrace is used three or four evenings a week for fellowship and lessons in scripture." Then adding a thought, he said, "You will be a marvelous new teaching resource." He was guiding them toward the house and the welcome promise of nourishment.

As they ate, Prisca was full of questions. "Tell me about the Jerusalem Temple. I've heard that it is beautiful."

Barnabas nodded. "Its splendor may only be described in superlatives. There are hundreds of Levites serving as priest each day, and the large porticos are filled with teachers. The Gentile court is a marketplace that must be seen to believe it is so vast. During the festivals it is difficult to walk through, there are so many pilgrims." He would have added more but she interrupted.

"And is Jesus proclaimed in such splendor?"

A frown clouded Barnabas' face as he replied, "At first, yes. But then the High Priest took exception and had Peter arrested. That seemed to start the opposition. When James, the brother of John, was executed and Stephen stoned to death, the followers were chased out of the city, and the believers were rounded up like enemies." A shocked expression was on his listeners' faces.

"I recall as we were entering Jerusalem for Passover," he continued, "the Pharisees ordered Jesus to silence the people who were shouting, 'Hosanna! Blessed is he who comes in the name of the Lord!' Jesus replied that if the people were silenced, even the stones would cry out in greeting." Barnabas had his engaging grin as the memory warmed his heart.

"Then you were with him the whole time?" Prisca asked.

"No, I was on a journey from Cyprus to Jerusalem when my attention was captured by a crowd of people in Capernaum. Jesus was teaching at the home of Simon Peter. I stopped to listen. He was saying that he hadn't come to destroy the Law, but to fulfill it. Four men worked their way through the crowd carrying a paralyzed friend lying on his pallet. Because of the press of people, they could not get to Jesus, so they went up on the roof and made a hole in the tiles. They lowered the man down to Jesus." He shook his head still amazed at what he had seen. "Jesus told the man that his sins were forgiven; that he should take his pallet and walk. And the man did!" Barnabas nodded his head vigorously. "I became a follower from that day."

With excitement Prisca asked Mark, "And were you with him then?"

"No, I wasn't introduced to the living Lord. Barnabas is my mother's brother. He arranged for Jesus and the twelve Apostles to use the terrace on our home for the Passover feast. That was the night Jesus was arrested. But I was with them three days later when the resurrected Lord stood before us and told us to go out and teach, to make disciples, and to baptize them." The young man wore the same grin.

Barnabas added, "When the temple guards came to his house in search of Jesus, we were terrified. But this brave lad had heard the apostles say they were going to Gethsemane to pray. While we stood in shock, Mark ran to warn them. He got there just as the melee was happening and was fortunate to lose only his tunic."

Those words caused the listeners to seek more information.

Instead, Mark told them, "I spent two summers writing the memory accounts of the Apostles. They are some experiences we must never forget. But unless we carefully write them into a record, after so many astounding moments with Jesus, some begin to fade from our thoughts. Before I could put the final touches on the scroll, we had a successful mission across Cyprus. A former Pharisee named Saul of Tarsus had a life-changing encounter with the risen Lord on the road to Damascus. Now he is known as Paul and claims the risen Lord commanded him to be a light to the Gentiles. Barnabas went with him to lower Galatia, and I went with Thomas, one of the twelve, to the cities of Decapolis."

The lamps were burning low; and the food tray was empty. It was time for rest, but Prisca still had questions to ask. "I surely want to hear more about that tunic, but I am more curious about your families. How are your wives managing with you gone for such long periods?" Her direct gaze suggested this was a question that must be answered.

Barnabas said, "Neither of us has had the opportunity to marry. My sister was the last surviving relative of mine, and her husband, Silas, is even now on a mission with the former Pharisee."

"I have no brothers or sisters," Mark added. "Perhaps my father's absence of half of each year for the governor precluded more children."

Softly Prisca said, "That is a great sacrifice. Your love of the Lord God must be great. We must talk more about this after you are rested. I am especially concerned about the amount of time we get to have you here in Ephesus. There seems to be a deep yearning here for knowledge about the Lord God, and Jesus his son. I hope you can enlighten us."

Mark had been aware that Aquila had asked no questions during their conversation. On the way out to the tent, he asked Barnabas, "Did her fragrance remind you of pomegranate blossoms?"

Barnabas had a slight smile as he answered, "I'm not sure. I was trying to decide if her eyes are light brown or grey."

Somewhere nearby a rooster irritatingly greeted the morning, prodding Mark out of a sound sleep. His second thought, after blessing the rooster, was the word of the Psalmist: "This is the day that the Lord has made! I will rejoice and be glad in it!" He also heard the voices of laborers offloading the hides. He was sure he could help them and gain some needed exercise. As soon as he had taken care of morning duties, he joined them.

The other two wagon drivers recognized the guest of their employer. They cheerily welcomed his help. Mark was actually surprised at the weight of the tanned leather, but did his best not to struggle as each was lifted off the wagon. By the time they were all carefully sorted and stacked in the warehouse, he was perspiring heavily and ready for a bit of rest.

He had just washed up a bit and pulled on his other tunic when Mark heard a child's voice call from the front of the tent, "Mama says breakfast is ready. You can join us if you want. The workers are already there and devotions are about to begin." Both Barnabas and Mark hurried into a fresh surprise of the day.

Their hosts sang a song that was new to the visitors. Then Prisca shared a prayer: "Gracious Heavenly God, Creator of all that is and is to be, we praise you for this new morning, for bodies rested and alert. We praise you for the gift of knowledge that is eager to be shared with others. Use us this day as vessels of mercy in league with all your heavenly beings, that we might prosper in your grace. Amen." Her voice was warm and clear, so easy to understand; but Mark was unaccustomed to hear a woman take such a leadership role. He would need to speak with his uncle about this unusual situation. Perhaps it was acceptable in the province of Asia.

Another unfamiliar song was sung. Then Aquila read from a fragment of a scroll: "Hear the words of the prophet Isaiah. 'Do you not know? Have you not heard? The Lord is the everlasting God, the Creator of the ends of the earth. He will not grow tired or weary, and his understanding no one can fathom. He gives strength to the weary and increase of power to the weak. Even youths grow tired and weary, and young men stumble and fall; but those who hope in the Lord will renew their strength. They will soar on wings like eagles; they will run and not grow weary, they will walk and not be faint.'"

He gently rolled the scroll and placed it on the table. With a smile he said, "Today will be a busy one for us. We must finish the three travel tents for the Macedonians, and there are two Saracens coming to look at the display tent. They suggested they might want six or eight of the large style." Looking at Barnabas he added, "It is not necessary for you to remove your traveling bags. They make the tent look livable." Then looking at everyone, Aquila said, "Tonight we will have a special fellowship to welcome our missionaries. There will be food for everyone, and the terrace will be a joyous place." Spreading wide his hands he concluded, "Amen."

The food trays were of immediate interest.

When the workers were off to their individual tasks, Prisca told the travelers that Sarah, who does the laundry, would be glad to include their soiled tunics.

"You might want to be free from the stains of your journey." Her smile was a morning blessing.

Aquila added to it by saying, "Alban told me that you volunteered to help unload the hides. He said that your labor has caused him to consider joining the evening fellowship. He has never seen a missionary who is willing to use his back before he uses his mouth. Your witness was well received by hm." He gave a hardy pat on Mark's shoulder. It was going to be an interesting day.

About the third hour of the morning, Barnabas and Mark were on the terrace planning their evening. They noticed a group of men enter the gate, led by Alban. Dressed in unusual robes and turbans, the group made their way to the display tent and were inside for several minutes. Aquila joined them, and after a bit they walked around the tent inspecting it closely. There was considerable conversation, even some arm waving. Then Aquila walked back to the warehouse, and Alban walked out the gate with the group. Apparently the buyers were not pleased with what they saw. The missionaries went back to planning their approach for the fellowship.

Mark said, "You do a better job with the initial announcement that the age of fulfillment has dawned. A new order is being inaugurated, and these people are being invited to join in the new community. Since you were with Jesus, you also do a very convincing account that this new age has come through the life, death and resurrection of Jesus Christ, all of which are in direct fulfillment of the prophecies of the scriptures. They are the result of the plan and foreknowledge of God."

Barnabas nodded his agreement.

Then he said, "You, however, are gifted at presenting the promise that these events will soon reach their completion in the return of Christ in glory and judgment of the living and the dead. You have the teachings that Jesus used in making that clear. That will lead naturally into an appeal for repentance, and the offer of forgiveness and the Holy Spirit, and the promise of eternal life." Both men smiled in agreement. "It is a very workable and complete plan. Let's pray about it."

Over a light noon meal of boiled fish, bread and figs, the missionaries enjoyed the hospitality of the family. Prisca was happy to have an opportunity to introduce her daughters Phoebe and Daphne. "It was Daphne who wanted to wake you and call you to breakfast. You had already put in a morning's work."

Aquila explained, "We also have a son, Justinian, who decided when we had to leave Rome that he would remain with his grandfather. He has a lovely canyon meadow near Ortona, east of Rome where he raises oxen. Justinian is the reliable supplier of hides for our business. My father is still in good health but appreciative of the help he is receiving, and so am I."

Reminded of the tent business, Mark asked, "We noticed the Saracens examined the tent, but left without purchasing."

Aquila chuckled, "They'll return. Their idea was to intimidate me into a lower price. I told Alban to guide them to the tentmaker Simeon, not far from here. I told them if they were in the market for cheap tents they must go elsewhere. They very much approved of our tent with double-stitched seams and enforced finished edges. Now they know they must pay a fair price for it too. There were only two who first talked with me; now there are five. I think they are purchasing to resell at a profit."

Prisca wanted to change the subject to the fellowship time this evening. "I noticed the songs we chose this morning are not ones you use. Tell me some of the songs we can share together." Overhead the sun heated the air, and on the terrace their growing friendship warmed their hearts.

The Saracens returned by the ninth hour and, after lengthy haggling, agreed to purchase a dozen tents. That sizeable order would tax Aquila's inventory and hide supply. Perhaps he would need to include the display tent.

The sun had not quite set, but long shadows were sneaking across the compound. As many as thirty men and a dozen women were gathered on the terrace for food and fellowship. Aquila seemed to know them all by name. A few came over to introduce themselves; they had heard that Barnabas was even one who had travelled with Jesus.

Phoebe strummed a lyre, which gathered folks' attention as it set the pitch and tempo. Prisca started the song of praise: "Come bless the Lord, all ye servants of the Lord, who stand by night in the house of the Lord! Lift up your hands to the holy place and bless the Lord! May the Lord bless you from Zion, he who made heaven and earth!" As the concluding phrase was repeated many raised their hands and increased their volume. There was good spirit in this gathering. They sang another song and Prisca offered a prayer.

"Glorious Creator of the land and sea, Designer of every realm, we are grateful for your presence and the great teaching that will come this evening. We are the people who love you and long to serve you faithfully. Here now, we present our hearts and minds for your service. Amen." If her leadership was unusual, Mark was aware of its blessing. He was grateful for the purity of it.

After an introduction, Barnabas did an elaborate explanation of the importance of this evening and the enormous decision that could be made. "You can choose to be one of the Master's followers, his chosen disciple." All were holding their breath for what was to follow.

Mark stood and said nothing for a long while, just looking into the eyes of the listeners. Finally he said, "When the Son of man comes in his glory, and all the angels with him, then he shall sit on his glorious throne. Before him will be gathered all the nations, and he will separate them one from another as a shepherd separates the sheep from the goats, and he will place the sheep at his right hand, but the goats at the left.

"Then the King will say to those at his right hand, 'Come, O blessed of my Father, inherit the kingdom prepared for you from the foundation of the world; for I was hungry and you gave me food, I was thirsty and you gave me drink, I was a stranger and you welcomed me, I was naked and you clothed me, I was sick and you visited me, I was in prison and you came to me. Then the righteous will answer him, 'Lord, when did we see thee hungry and feed thee, or thirsty and give thee drink? And when did we see thee a stranger and welcome thee, or naked and clothe thee? And when did we see thee sick or in prison and visit thee?' And the King will answer them, 'Truly, I say to you, as you did it to one of the least of these my brethren, you did it to me.'

"Then he will say to those at his left hand, 'Depart from me, you cursed, into the eternal fire prepared for the devil and his angels; for I was hungry and you gave me no food, I was thirsty and you gave me no drink, I was a stranger and you did not welcome me, naked and you did not clothe me, sick and in prison and you did not visit me.' Then they will answer, 'Lord, when did we see thee hungry or thirsty or a stranger or naked or sick or in prison, and did not minister to thee?' Then he will answer them, 'Truly, I say to you, as you did it not to one of the least of these, you did it not to me.' And they will go away into eternal punishment, but the righteous into eternal life.' These are the words of Jesus, our Lord."

After a long pause, Mark said, "Now if these words hurt, and you were aware of your transgressions, I am not surprised, for we have all sinned and fallen short of the glory of God. We have all ignored the opportunity to minister to the poor or show mercy. The good news is that through the sacrifice made on the cross, Jesus Christ has made a way for us to be made right with God and receive complete forgiveness of those sins. Jesus has invited us to be baptized, to be washed whiter than snow, and to receive his Spirit. Who here this evening would like that baptism? Who would be free from the bonds of sin's guilt and receive God's righteousness?"

Nearly every hand raised, much to his surprise and joy.

"Aquila, as they kneel will you stand behind them and say their name for me?"

A pitcher of water from the table was sufficient to pour a spoonful on each bowed head. So began a monumental moment for the fellowship of Ephesus. Again and again after saying their name Mark spoke these words: "You are baptized in the name of Jesus the Christ; your sins are forgiven and your name is written in the book of life." His voice broke when he came to Prisca with Phoebe on one side and Daphne on the other. When they had gone all around the circle, Aquila knelt before him and received the same blessing.

Barnabas stood and said, "Jesus would not want you to leave this time of dedication without receiving a final blessing. If you have an illness, he wants to heal you. If you have a broken friendship because angry words have been spoken, he wants to reconcile you. If you have anxiety because the future is unclear, he wants to calm your fears. If your body is weary from work, know that in this night he will give you comfort and refreshed strength. Receive now the load-lifting, life-changing blessing of Christ Jesus our Lord. Amen."

They sang three more songs before folks began to leave. Nearly every person wanted to express gratitude for a renewed sense of joyful understanding and hope.

When the terrace had cleared except for the missionaries and Aquila's family, Prisca said softly, "I hoped it would be that good! I have longed for witnesses who could bring us both devotion and sound teaching. The baptism was a perfect new beginning. Did you hear them say they hope you can be here tomorrow evening again?" She looked into the eyes of Barnabas and Mark. "I hope you can. I feel this is a season for Godliness in Ephesus."

In fact they worked out a schedule whereby the terrace was filled to overflowing on Sunday, Wednesday and Friday. Barnabas made them feel welcomed and part of a bold new movement of God's people. Mark told them stories of miraculous healings and signs of power. "Jesus fed a multitude having only five loaves of bread to set before them and they picked up twelve baskets of pieces left over." He told of Jesus' courage in the face of opposition of the Pharisees; when challenged Jesus asked them, 'Which is easier to say, 'Your sins are forgiven' or 'take up your pallet and walk?' He described the Passover supper Jesus shared with his disciples, and initiated a service of Holy Communion. Just as with the baptism, the believers wanted communion regularly. He taught them the believer's prayer, and most importantly the baptism of the Holy Spirit.

One spring morning, Barnabas announced that it was time for them to move on to Smyrna. "We are overly fond of you and your gracious hospitality," he said to Aquila. To Prisca, he said, "Both Mark and I have become dependent upon your goodness. Your fellowship is growing and quite prepared to continue without us. Mark has written notes from every gathering so you can reread and discuss the things we talked about. It's time." It was also time for tears.

In the morning before dawn as the two stepped out of the display tent they found their hosts waiting for them. Prisca handed them a bag with enough bread, cheese and figs to last a couple of days. Aquila offered a pouch filled with coins.

"The fellowship took an offering to ensure that you would have sufficient funds to begin in Smyrna."

Barnabas removed two coins from the pouch and returned it to him saying, "This will be plenty for us. Perhaps the fellowship might choose some worthy person in need who will be blessed as we have been."

Prisca embraced them both dearly, saying, "You have changed our lives eternally." She was weeping as she turned away.

Something like that scenario happened again and again as they made their way through the mission, although there were no folks who could match Aquila and Prisca. The missionaries were in Smyrna and Pergamum for over six months each; Thyatira and Sardis were less than that, and Philadelphia was almost eight months. The fellowship at Laodicea struggled for two months before the duo knew they had been unsuccessfull in their best try. All in all they spent three years before returning to the inn at Didyma.

Yet Again in Confirmation Class

Shelly reported that her mom was going to miss confirmation classes. "She said the house was going to be noisier for one thing, and especially that she would miss hearing about the information we had talked about in class."

Pastor Randle said, "This is our last class before you join the church. I promised to give you nine reasons how being a believer is going to make you a better person. I'm glad I was told about this when I was your age. Sometimes it is easy for teenagers to feel unsure of themselves; sometimes they feel left out, or that no one likes them. These nine reasons are going to make you a more fulfilled student today. If you continue with these nine fruits of the Spirit, you will be a better person a year from now. The wonderful truth is it will continue to bless you when you are an adult and every year after that. Pretty cool, huh? How would you like to know that you have the tools to be right with God, right with the people around you, as well as happy with yourself?

"That's probably enough hype. Look at the page I handed out. It's a copy of page 1787 of your study Bible: Galatians 5:16 ff called 'Life by the Spirit.' I'm reading just verses 22 and 23." When he was sure everyone had the page, he read, "'But the fruit of the Spirit is love, joy, peace, patience, kindness, goodness, faithfulness, gentleness and self-control. Against such things there is no law.' Those are nine flowers that help you bloom into a wonderful person.

"I found it useful to think of these as three groups of three. The first three virtues produce a beautiful relationship between you and God: love, joy, and peace. The first one, love, has four words in Greek: there is romantic passionate love called *Eros*, which is never used in scripture; there is brotherly (sisterly) love like love of your school or patriotic love. That's *philia*. There is family love, how you feel about your folks some of the time, or your Grandmother all the time. That's *storge*. *Agape* is the word that is used here for the word 'love'. It is the unfailing, amazing way God loves us. It means that no matter what happens to us by way of insult or humiliation, we will never seek anything but the highest good for that person. This is the very core of forgiveness. It is therefore a feeling of the mind as much as the heart; it involves the will as much as our emotions, which we can only do with the help of God.

"Joy is sort of the same thing. It is not the joy we feel when we get what we asked for at Christmas, or the joy we might feel if we could beat Skyline this year. It is the contentment of knowing that we already have everything we need to live a full and happy life and that God will supply whatever more we might need."

"Peace is another difficult word which means so much more than the end of warfare. In Hebrew the word *Shalom* means more than the absence of trouble; it refers to everything that makes for someone's highest and very best good. So when love, joy, and peace are nurtured in our garden, the produce is pleasing to both us and God.

"The next three are very nutritious for us and others around us: patience, kindness and goodness. Patience is another of those difficult to understand words. It sort of means the grace of someone who has been wronged and chooses not to retaliate or take revenge; someone who is slow to anger or show wrath. It's interesting that in scriptures it is a common word to describe the attitude God and Jesus have toward people. God bears with our sinfulness and refuses to cast us away. If we learn to model that same spirit into our lives we will have many opportunities to practice forbearance, forgiveness and patience with others, much to their relief and ours.

"Kindness and goodness are such similar words they are frequently interchangeable.

But there is a difference; goodness can rebuke, correct or discipline. Jesus was good when he cleansed the temple and drove out those who were treating it like a bazaar. He was kind to the sinning woman who anointed his feet. We need the goodness that at one and the same time can be kind and strong. The person who will grow these in her or his life will be a blessing to those folks who share their life."

Pastor Randle took a breath and said, "We are almost through the list. The final three virtues are faithfulness, gentleness and self control; when they grow in our garden, we are the ones who are most blessed. Faithfulness is usually thought about as marital fidelity, but it is so much more than that. It's a common Greek word for trustworthy. It is the characteristic of someone who is reliable. Doesn't that sound like the sort of person you want to be?

"Gentleness is a hard word to translate. It could mean submissive to the will of God. It could also mean someone who is teachable, someone who is not too proud to learn. Most often in scripture it means someone who is considerate; before they rush to judgment they consider the back-story. Do you remember the old saying: before judging a person you should walk a mile in her moccasins first? A considerate person is gentle.

"The last one on our list this afternoon is self-control. I like the definition as someone who is only angry at the right time and never angry at the wrong time. It is the ability to master our appetite for pleasure, which is the only way we can be fit to be a servant of others. Those nine virtues are all fruit of the Spirit at work in our lives, making us right with God, with others and with ourselves."

Danny whispered just loud enough for all his classmates to hear, "Mom made spiced applesauce cupcakes. My self-control is just about worn out. Is it time for snacks?"

Return to Didyma

It was late afternoon when they arrived at the inn. Barnabas had made several suggestions of what they could do in the event the Inn was either filled, or closed. Mark, however, was confident they would be welcomed. His optimism was difficult for his uncle to share after the frustrating two years they had just finished after Ephesus.

"Uncle, where is your faith? I know we were spoiled in Ephesus, but there were many successes since then. We must overlook those who found it easy to compromise their belief with sinful pleasures. We must pray that their heart, and yours, might be revived to one that pleases God more," Mark said jovially.

Trying to match the younger man's mood, Barnabas said, "A visit to my homeland would revive my heart. Yes, we are returning to Jerusalem, but a short visit to Paphos would allow me to worship with friends who do not also worship the Emperor or the priestesses of Artemis. If we go by ship, we will probably stop in Cyprus anyway." His voice was more serious than usual. Mark realized how draining the past two years had been on his uncle, who had tried to hide the strain.

In an attempt at humor, Mark said, "Perhaps we could find Elymas to see if he has regained his sight. It might be that he needs a healing touch."

Barnabas was beyond the effect of Mark's lightness. He said quietly, "Let's see if we can find the innkeeper, or see if he even remembers you."

Not only did they find him, they found a dining room filled with men, many of them wearing swords, but all dining comfortably with one another. Luscious saw them enter and hurried to greet them. "Oh, Mr. John, it makes me happy to see you again. It has been over two years since your father was last here. May I prepare a dinner for you?" He could tell by Mark's questioning gaze that an explanation was more important at the moment.

"It was your father's suggestion. The Roman garrison provides food for the officers, but it is only marginal. Your father suggested offering a subscription to fifty of them. They pay once a month and eat here as often as they like. As you can see it is orderly and efficient. We removed three sleeping rooms to make more table space. It is genius. We are safe in their presence, and they are happy with the food and wine we serve." As he was showing them to an empty table he added, "The room will be empty soon. Then I need to talk to you privately."

As they enjoyed bowls of hardy lamb stew, more spicy than they expected, fresh bread and wine that had far less water than usual, Mark said softly, "No wonder the officers want to eat here. It is delicious. If I ate like this every day I would not be able to bend over to tie my sandals." He had been smiling since they entered the inn.

"I wonder what news Luscious has for you," Barnabas murmured. His attitude hadn't changed either, so he had no smile. "Perhaps the Romans are going to confiscate the inn."

"And perhaps it is news from my father. Good news that will lift your glum mood. It is possible that we haven't spent enough time in prayer. You said a number of times that our task is to faithfully present the word of God. We did that! Do you not believe that God will be able to magnify our work just as he did the loaves broken for the multitude?" His gaze was direct and purely positive.

His uncle nodded and tried to manage a smile. "You are right, I know. I'm having trouble overlooking the casual contempt the Laodiceans had for our efforts." His head shook in disgust.

"You told me yourself that their response is not upon us. Perhaps the future will find that they eventually understood and repented. It is God's business, not ours."

Barnabas didn't say anything, just nodded his head in agreement.

By the time their bowls were emptied and the last piece of bread consumed, the other tables were emptied and cleared. They were alone with Luscious, who finally sat down with them and asked, "May I speak confidentially with you?" The question was directed to Mark but his gaze was on Barnabas.

Mark replied, "Barnabas is my father's brother in law. He has the same authority as I do. You may speak freely to us."

Luscious took a deep breath, then said, "Your father has given me a large task to care for his various interests during his absence. Until now it has been a simple matter, and it could continue in the same manner. The man who has been renting the vineyard in Gadara, however, wants to purchase it and has made a second very attractive offer. He will continue to rent if that is his only recourse. Secondly the large property adjacent here to the inn, just up the hill, is in distress and is available for sale. He has just lowered his price again. With your approval, I will exchange the vineyard for the villa that can become rooms rented to retired Roman soldiers. The income from them would be much more dependable than wine making, with obvious benefits. They could become a secondary set of diners in the inn. It seems to me this would be very beneficial to your father's holdings." He looked into Mark's eyes, waiting for a response.

"Uncle what do you think about the idea on first hearing?" Mark asked. "I was never fond of the vineyard. We were given little choice to move there. So I think I am in favor of consolidating his holdings here. Do you have any thoughts?"

Barnabas answered with a shrug, "Without knowing the true value of either property, I suppose I would defer to your father's initial trust in this man. Silvanus…Silas, gave his signet to Luscious. If he trusted him that much, I suppose I do too."

"That's exactly my thought," Mark agreed. Looking at the innkeeper, he added, "Luscious, I have no idea what financial arrangements you have with my father. I do not want to alter those at all. It does seem, however, that the situation is changing in ways that your first agreement could not foresee. Let us, you and me, agree that from now on you keep an accurate account, recording the profits you make here, on all transactions. We will divide those equally. Neither of us may become wealthy, or perhaps we both will, but in any event we will receive the same. Do you agree?"

The innkeeper's mouth moved but no sound came out. He tried again, "Mr. John, sir, you are as generous as your father. It will be my honor, sir, to be your partner. I vow that you will not be disappointed." His hand trembled as Mark shook it in confirmation.

"I do not know where our journeys will take us," the young man said with a smile, "but from now on I will consider Didyma my home. Perhaps I may have a small room along with the old soldiers." He clapped the innkeeper's shoulder affectionately.

Two days later they boarded a coastal freighter bound for Paphos. Two days after that they were enjoying fellowship with many of the believers they had met years before. In the glow of singing and prayers they agreed to meet again at the sixth hour in the city forum, which would be large and open to the public. It would be an opportunity for both Barnabas and Mark to share God's word and inspire these folks once again. The two prayed into the night and first thing in the morning. Finally Barnabas felt that he could genuinely smile.

Grief!

In the morning the praise continued. There were songs and prayers before hospitality. The two missionaries agreed that the teamwork that had served them for three years would be just right. Barnabas would remind the crowd of the prophecies that beckoned in a new day of faith. He would offer the invitation to become part of the new era of God's grace by proclaiming the passion and victorious resurrection of Jesus. Through two or three teaching stories of Jesus, Mark would stress the urgency of choice and invite the listeners to present their hearts and minds afresh. They were satisfied with the plan and eager to be back in Paphos.

When the hour arrived they found their way to the forum, a large circular space with colonnades on one end. A group of folks were already singing songs of faith. Mark was surprised that fifty or sixty men were already there, and more were gathering. A rather short man wearing a blue and white scarf asked if he could stand in front of Mark.

"The tall men look right over me and push me out of their way." To prove that he was having trouble seeing, his head moved from side to side as he peered around the one in front of him. Barnabas was getting into his presentation, more and more expressive of the prophecies of the Messiah.

"Perhaps you should move closer, where there are fewer to block you," Mark advised.

"No," the diminutive man answered. "I think it will be all right if you agree not to trample me." He paused and then asked, "Are you with the speaker?"

A startled alarm rippled through Mark, but then he realized that many had seen the two missionaries together in the past. "He is my uncle. We are just back from the region of Pergamum."

Barnabas announced that a fresh new day of God's grace was dawning and all were welcome to join.

The short man pulled a blue and white scarf from his robe saying, "If you wear this it will keep you safe....from the sun." He moved a bit too close to Mark, who backed up a half pace.

Another ripple of anxiety shot through Mark. "No, thank you. The sun and I are good friends." He pushed the scarf back into the man's hands.

The man moved too close again as he said, "You know, there was a time I was just as tall as you, four cubits. But two summers in the hot sun took a toll on me. Now I am barely three cubits. Please wear it for your protection." Mark backed up a bit more, noticing two other men nearby pull blue and white scarves onto their heads. Something was about to happen. He covered his head with the scarf just as someone near Barnabas shouted "Blasphemy! He is uttering blasphemy!"

There was a sudden surge of angry men targeting Barnabas. Clubs were suddenly swinging and fists flailing. Mark started to lunge to his uncle's defense but the short man grasped him with a vice-like grip.

"I could only save one of you. I'm sorry." He was directing Mark toward the edge of the crowd with urgency, as the young man saw the flash of a dagger pulled from the sleeve of an attacker. The angry blade slashed through logic and mercy to find its victim. Barnabas grasped his chest; bright red blood gushing from the assassin's wound.

"Jesus is Lor...." was the final cry of the man who had only encouraged others. In a crumpled lifeless heap Barnabas fell to the ground.

Mark's brain seemed numb, but he heard the quiet instructions of the short man say, "Go with these men to the *Ianthe*. We sail with the tide. If you remain here, you and many of your followers will not survive." At least a dozen men all wearing blue and white scarves surrounded him as they hurried toward the harbor.

Mark stumbled down the cobble-stone street, his eyesight blurred by tears. Several minutes passed before the sob erupted from his chest.

It was unbelievable to him that Barnabas was gone, slain by a Hebrew. Where was the sense in it? Another wracking sob spilled tears down his face. The men stopped at a sleek ship moored to the main dock. They encouraged him to hurry aboard and go to the cabin below the steering deck. Once inside and alone, Mark wept like a child.

Unpaid Debt

In an office near the city center, the short man was speaking with a robed Pharisee. Their conversation had degraded from cordial business to confrontational. The Pharisee had just said, "I care little for your agreement. Your ship will return to Joppa when our business here is concluded, and no sooner." His stare was cold.

"Our agreement was to deliver you and your thugs from Joppa to Paphos, end of contract. Your payment will be immediate and in gold," the short man said softly.

The Pharisee waved his hand at the man who still wore his blue and white scarf. "You will be paid at my decision, which is when we are prepared to return."

"You are making a dangerous mistake. Pay me, and I will leave peacefully."

"You will leave now. My guards will see to it, and I will contact you when it is time for our return." The Pharisee shifted his attention to a scroll on the table.

The short man walked to the door. When he opened it, he said simply, "Centurion, I need your assistance." The Pharisee looked up with a start. Four Roman soldiers came into the room quickly. The short man said, "His guards have threatened me, and this Jerusalem lawyer refuses to satisfy our contract. Throw him in jail until I am paid."

One of the guards stood to protect the Pharisee and was instantly knocked unconscious. The other two stood against the wall with their hands at their sides. The Pharisee had gone pale, muttering, "You cannot…" A rough hand grabbed him by the nap of his neck and forced him to the floor.

"Wait! Wait!" his thin voice nearly wept. "The payment is right here!" The Roman jerked him to his feet so he could produce the pouch of gold.

As the short man took the payment he said to the Roman, "This man and his butchers just assassinated a citizen in the forum only minutes ago. If you hurry you might catch the rest. This one is their leader." The four soldiers hurried out with the stunned Pharisee in tow.

The short man said to the two frightened guards who still stood against the wall, "You should have paid in the first place."

Mark, still in the cabin, was aware of heavy footsteps around and above him, but nothing made sense. He was awake but in a terrible nightmare. Once again wracking sobs were uncontrollable. When he could feel the rhythmic motion of the ship riding on the waves of the open ocean, Mark could finally sit up. But he remained on the cabin floor, asking himself how this monstrous thing could have happened.

Benbusiris

The cabin door opened and the short man entered. Mark struggled to his feet, but was not sure what to say. Finally he said, "Thank you for rescuing me." A sob bubbled out again.

"I think you said he was a relative. Is that correct?" the man asked with obvious respect.

"Yes, his name is Barnabas; he is…" he corrected himself, "He was my mother's brother. His birth name was Joseph, but the followers of Jesus nicknamed him 'son of encouragement.'" Another sob punctuated his voice.

"Then neither of you is the missionary called Paul, formerly a Pharisee in Jerusalem, with his assistant Silas?" the confused man asked.

Mark's head jerked up as he heard the name. "No, we were with them four years ago. Silas, whose Roman name is Silvanus, is my father." A cold wave of understanding shook him.

The short man nodded his understanding as well. "You were not the targets this day. The assassin mistook you two. How ironic that the brother-in-law took the knife instead." He walked over and gave a sympathetic pat on Mark's shoulder. "The Romans have the lead Pharisee and perhaps some of the others. It was the best I could do." He was quiet a moment. "The crew heard them talking about their plot to kill two missionaries. You must have been doing something that has frightened their order." After another long pause he said, "We decided to intervene. It would have been best if we could have saved you both. I am very happy to have you safe aboard the *Ianthe*."

"Where am I going?" Mark asked with no particular interest.

"We are returning to our home in Alexandria. I can arrange for your travel back to Jerusalem, although I have heard that is a very dangerous city right now. The Romans are less and less patient with the squabbles of the Hebrews. Emperor Caligula was about to put his own image in the Holy of Holies. Fortunately a more moderate Claudius has taken his place, but it is still a steaming pot. Perhaps we can find you work in Alexandria. Do you have any training?"

"I am a pretty good record keeper. I write well in both Hebrew and Greek." Mark was still in shock. His voice was without energy or interest and interrupted by gasps.

"How old are you, son?"

"I believe I am twenty-eight years old. It has been a while since anyone cared about that." Mark was trying to get back on his emotional feet. "I do have a partner in a Didyma inn and a villa that houses retired Roman soldiers there." If it was not quite true at least it was better than admitting that he was homeless and unemployed.

"Well now," the short man responded, understanding that even after such a narrow escape with his life, this young man was struggling to put up a wholesome façade. "Do you have any other assets?"

"My father owns several investment properties that are rented, and we have a financier who is caring for our accounts." He didn't want to say much more, but that much was factual to his knowledge.

"And you said your father's name is…?"

"He is called Silas by the Hebrews. His Greek name is Silvanus. He was Governor Pilate's Tribute Consul for the northern territories." That made the short man's eyebrows raise in surprise.

"My name is Benbusiris. I operate a number of coastal freighters. This is our flagship, the sleekest and fastest. We only transport prominent people who are in a hurry on *Ianthe*. If the wind holds steady, we will be in port in six days. During that time we have a guest cabin for you. You are welcome to tour the boat and meet the crew. Don't be surprised if they seem unfriendly. I have chosen them for their obedience and sea skills. To a man they volunteered to join in your rescue. That's the sort of loyalty they have. We will make sure you are comfortable, and perhaps we can talk more. I have some interest in religious matters. Did you know there are nearly a million Jews in Alexandria?" That made the young man's eyebrows raise in surprise.

Steady wind and calm seas allowed the sleek boat to make excellent time. On the afternoon of the fifth day, Benbusiris approached Mark on the deck.

"I hope you have had time for prayer to consider the path for your future. May I invite you to dine in my cabin? Christos tells me you have eaten only one meal each day." He waited for a reply.

"I have found solace in prayer" Mark quietly said. "While it still makes no sense to me, I can now accept the reality of Barnabas' death. He lived well, and he died faithfully. No man can ask for more." He studied the distant clouds and surmised that they were over Egypt.

Benbusiris asked patiently, "And have you found direction for yourself?"

"This may sound irresponsible to you; I have for several years believed that God's guidance is frequently offered as opportunity. I may not be able to see where the path leads, but an open door is the invitation to follow a holy will. If I am faithful in seeking that will, I believe my journey will prove inspiring."

"Come, sit in my cabin with me. Let me tell you about an opportunity." He turned and walked comfortably to the door. Mark had not acquired that easy gait on the canted deck, but he managed to weave his way there.

A Story of Sadness

Once seated, Benbusiris said, "It is odd that I can speak with businessmen with ease, and can negotiate or command, but when it comes to matters of my family I have difficulty sharing my thoughts. I have watched you for the days of our trip and you pray to your God, but not in anger or rage, but in praise. You grieve unlike anyone I have known. You sing praise songs to your Lord." He paused for so long Mark wondered if there was some response he expected. But the captain went on.

"Let me tell you about a great sorrow I have been carrying. My son's name was Barisis. He was what every father hopes for. He wanted to know the shipping business well enough that one day he could take my place. About five years ago he was going to Sparta on one of our boats whose captain was Mathias, his brother-in-law, my son-in-law. They were taking a load of figs to Sparta. It was a very routine trip." He paused to choose his words. "Somewhere between Rhodes and Crete, they were attacked by pirates. A bit of wreckage and two bodies washed up near Cnidus. The ship was eventually discovered abandoned in Sparta. After several months we accepted the fact that the boys were killed. My wife Sarah took their deaths so hard she became ill. A fever took her final strength. Some say she died of a broken heart." His face seemed pale and drawn.

Mark whispered, "I am so very sorry for your deep loss."

"The only reason I am telling you this is that the tragedy is not over. Mathias' wife is my only daughter, Ianthe. She has a five year old daughter named Oriana, who has never met her grandfather. Ianthe is still so in the grasp of awful grief, I'm afraid for her health. Whenever I try to talk with her, she is reminded of Barisis, a brother whom she loved dearly. She is face to face with the entire tragedy and breaks into sobbing tears. It has been over a year since we last spoke. I don't know what to do. I have hired a housekeeper and a cook for her so she is not alone. They report to me that she rarely speaks and frequently weeps."

"Benbusiris," Mark said softly, "what can I do to help you?"

"I have waited all day, hoping you would ask that. Here comes an opportunity, I believe you called it." He looked deeply into Mark's eyes. "I want to hire you to manage my affairs. You must know I don't need another to do this. I simply want to bring you in so Ianthe can be aware of you. You can have time to visit the Jewish synagogues, spread the good news, do whatever you want. It must, however, in some way affect Ianthe. You can meet her under the excuse of fixing her house or paying her debts. I want you to pray for her, with her if possible. Tell her stories of Jesus' miracles." His hand came down heavily on the table, making Mark jump in alarm. "I am so very worried about her. Help me."

"We can do that," Mark said reaching his hand across the table, gently grasping Benbusiris'. "We can pray right now." He bowed and said "Master of Heaven, Lord of Hosts, in the midst of a raging storm you commanded the wind and waves to be still and they obeyed. In the midst of the storm of anxiety and grief we call upon your peace. Hold us gently in your hand that our hearts might be encouraged and our fears put to rest. We come to you now that you may make us able to walk in your light; to act in your strength, to think in your wisdom, to speak in your truth, to live in your love, that when all the days are done, we may come to dwell in your glory. Now in the splendor of this day, I lift to you Benbusiris and Ianthe for comfort. Calm their fears, Lord, and lift their eyes above the ugly shadows of death. Let them see this day in all of your amazing grace, we ask in the holy name and power of Jesus, our Lord. So be it." The room was quiet except for the creaking of the vessel and the rush of water against the hull.

"What did you do to me?" the captain asked. "I feel lighter, less anxious. Did you cast a spell on me?"

Mark chuckled, "No, sir. We prayed for the peace of Christ Jesus and you have received it. It is truly not very complicated. God wants to bless you, and fill your cup to overflowing. He wants to replace your grief with joy."

"Do you really believe that?" the short man asked. His eyes studied Mark's features.

"With all my heart," the young man answered. "I have seen the wonder of it hundreds of times."

"If that happens, I'll pay you handsomely." Benbusiris was struggling to get back in control of his feelings.

Once again Mark chuckled, "I'm not interested in your money. It's your eternal soul I care about. Jesus came to us so we may have life, he said, and have it abundantly. That's what is at stake here."

The most pleasant words Mark heard his host speak were the next ones: "Mark, tell me about Jesus." They were together for several hours.

A New Land and Another Journey

By mid-day *Ianthe* was securely moored among the other Benbusiris ships. Mark accompanied him through the office spaces and then to his lavish home nearby. It seemed cavernous and empty with just one man living there. Mark was shown Barisis' room, which still had a stack of neatly folded linen tunics. He was told that he could make use of it and stay as long as he liked.

"I hope you will not be insulted by this offer," his host said, "but to tell the truth, your woven tunic is not very fresh. It smells like you have worn it for many miles. Please try on one of these. I think you will find that it fits and is much more comfortable on this warm day." He was also given a travelling bag complete with a small pouch of coins. A bowl of water with a cloth to use to cleanse his body was a welcomed and refreshing duty.

When he came out of the room his host was waiting with a woman. "This is Marissa, our cook. She will guide you to the home of Ianthe. It is not very far, perhaps five stadia. When you get back, we can eat and plan for tomorrow."

Mark felt like his day was out of his control and not getting any better in the future. He was, however, well into the opportunity that had been presented.

The house they eventually approached was a weary, nondescript home with a gate that opened to an equally neglected inner court. Marissa simply opened the door, calling, "'Anthe, it's Marissa, and I have a guest from your father as well as dinner." She waited near the door and then called again a bit louder, "Anthe, it's Marissa." Mark heard shuffling from the back.

A young woman entered the main room with a child in tow. They both had hair that hadn't been combed recently, and their robes hadn't been washed for an even longer time. They were both barefooted and for just a second, Mark remembered the first time he had seen Prisca running to meet him. This was so different. There was an emptiness in both of them.

"What may I do for you, sir," she asked without looking at him.

"Ianthe, ma'am, your father asked me to find out if your home has need for any repairs, or if there are any debts that require attention."

Now Ianthe looked at Mark, but not with a welcoming expression. She was aware of his brown eyes, strong square jaw, and muscular build. "Abba sent you to look in on his invalid daughter? I would think he could come up with a more reasonable excuse. You must be low on his list of workers." Her voice wasn't abrasive, simply empty of emotion.

"Ma'am, I heard only a tiny bit of the great sadness that has come to you. I wanted to come to your house and meet you."

"Your words are nice, but I suspect that father had to threaten you to get you here today."

"I'm sorry you feel that way. I can assure you that I am here out of gratitude, not obligation. One week ago on the island of Cyprus, your father and his crew rescued me from an assassination attempt that took the life of my uncle. He smuggled me aboard *Ianthe* and eventually brought me here. I owe him a great debt, which has nothing to do with this visit." His eyes held hers in a tender gaze.

"Are you telling me he has named one of his ships after me?" Her surprise was genuine.

"Is that news to you? It is his pride and joy, the sleekest fast coastal cruiser ever." Mark wasn't sure if she was accepting his words.

"What do you do for my father? You certainly don't sound like a sailor."

"I told him that I am a book-keeper, which is true. But I am also a missionary, building the fellowship of God's son, Messiah Jesus." His words were soft and warm.

"If he hears about that, I think you won't be his friend at all. He has no time for religion." She actually had a tiny flash of spunk.

"Oh, he knows about my calling. Yesterday we spent several hours speaking about God and the history of the Hebrew people. I believe he has a new appreciation for God's loving grace."

Ianthe started to say something more, but her lips closed tightly on the words.

Mark took a half step closer to her and said quietly, "I am praying that God will lift this great burden of grief from you and allow your heart to bloom with joy. Isn't that the meaning of your name, 'flower?' I will be glad to chat with you about that any time you wish. You see Marissa each day; she can bring me a message." Mark thought he had said enough for this first meeting.

He was correct and Ianthe understood his sensitive perception. It took a while before Merissa had a message to share.

The Gospel in Egypt

Benbusiris informed Mark about two synagogues that met within an easy walking distance. Mark visited the Sabbath evening meeting first. He chose to stand in the back without offering to speak. He felt that being so far from Jerusalem there might be a different style and custom. He was correct and glad he had chosen the more gentle introduction. By his third visit to each meeting, he was asked to speak, and did so with tact and immediate effect.

The reading from the Law was carefully shared: "You shall not hate your brother in your heart, but you shall reason with your neighbor, lest you bear sin because of him. You shall not take vengeance or bear any grudge against the sons of your own people, but you shall love your neighbor as yourself. I am the Lord."

Comments were invited, so Mark raised his hand. When he was acknowledged he said, "One day rabbi Jesus was teaching when a teacher of the law asked him which commandment might be the greatest." Several shrugged, understanding the trap being laid. "Jesus said the greatest commandment is the first: 'You shall love the Lord your God with all your heart and soul, mind and strength.'" Several more heads nodded in agreement. "Then Jesus added, 'A second is like it; you shall love your neighbor as yourself.' The lawyer wanted to justify himself for he believed that Jesus had answered properly. 'But who is my neighbor?' he asked."

"Jesus told this story, 'A certain man was going from Jerusalem down to Jericho. Bandits assaulted him, robbed him and left him for dead in the dirt at the side of the road. Now a priest came upon the scene but passed by on the other side of the road. So too a Levite passed by. Finally, a Samaritan came to where he was, and when he saw him, he had compassion, and went to him and bound up his wounds, pouring on oil and wine; then set him on his own beast and brought him to an inn and took care of him. And the next day he took out two silver coins and gave them to the innkeeper, saying, 'Take care of him and whatever more you spend, I will repay when I come back.'

"Jesus concluded by asking, 'Which of these three do you think proved neighbor to the man who fell among the robbers?' The man responded, 'The one who showed mercy on him.' And Jesus said to him, 'Go, and do likewise'."

Mark reminded the listeners of the guilt they had accumulated for failing to be a neighbor. He made it clear that only God can forgive sins, and the terrible cross and the sacrifice that was made upon it is the way mercy has already occurred. Several members asked him to return and tell them more about Jesus. Within two months he was no longer a stranger but a welcomed speaker. He wished his uncle could have enjoyed the growing interest and respect.

His acceptance from Ianthe was much less prominent. After their initial meeting she had waited almost a month before Marissa was asked to invite Mark back. Once again he found her unkempt and hollow. She asked what he and her father had talked about, but when he began to tell her, she rose and left the room. Several minutes passed before she returned, and it was apparent that she had been weeping. Mark had asked if he could pray for her, because the Lord whom he loved promised to seek and save the lost, even if they were lost in terrible grief. When Ianthe made no reply, he prayed a brief tender prayer for her comfort and peace.

Benbusiris praised Mark for his effort and acknowledged that there was hope for his daughter.

Two weeks later he had even better news. Ianthe had once again invited him to explain his work for her father and how it was that Mark managed to speak so often in the synagogues. The highlight of that visit was a small toy top that he had fashioned from a piece of wood and painted red and white. When the toy was spun on the table its whirling turned the colors rosy pink. Oriana was delighted and asked him to spin it again and again until he finally managed to get her to try it. That was the first time he was able to see Ianthe smile. It was a radiant moment. When Mark reported his progress to Benbusiris there was plenty of praise and happy emotion.

Marissa brought an invitation that was even more wonderful. Ianthe requested that both men join her for dinner. It was time Oriana met her grandfather. Just the invitation was enough to cause Benbusiris to weep and embrace Mark uncharacteristically.

"You told me that the power of God's love could lift the cloud of sorrow," Benbusiris, said in a whisper, "but I was too stubborn to think it was possible. I think this is a miracle. I praise you and your God."

When the dinner guests arrived at her home, they were pleased to find her long hair combed and held by a blue ribbon that accentuated her gray eyes. She wore a light blue tunic that was freshly cleaned. Oriana was dressed identically, and was still delighted with her spinning toy. Benbusiris thought his heart was going to burst with joy. He surprised them all by silently shedding a tear. Mark reached over and stroked his shoulder.

"Father," Ianthe asked, "this man who never seems to stop talking, told me that you saved his life. Is that true, or was he simply trying to impress me?" She smiled at both men.

Her father cleared his voice and said, "The damned Jews were after two other missionaries. As it turned out, one of them was Mark's father. The crew heard the assassins plotting the attack. I would have saved them both, but this one was the best I could do. Do you think I should throw him back?" It had been years since they had bantered like this.

"Is it also true that you put my name on one of your ships?" She was playfully indignant.

"It could have been one of the ugly fat freighters, but it is the most beautiful cruiser." After a moment he added, "I'm glad we had it at Paphos so we could pull this fellow out of a trap." Benbusiris reached over and rested his hand on Mark's shoulder.

She answered with a much more serious voice. "He is helping me out of a very deep hole. I don't even know how it is happening. He has never spoken Mathias' name, and yet we talked about the grief. It is not gone, of course, but today it feels manageable. And I'm even thinking about a tomorrow." Turning to face Mark she added, "I said to you that my life was over, and you just said, 'that previous life is over.' You told me I still get more."

Then looking at her father she said, "I realized that Oriana needs a mother; she needs a family. She needs something to believe in." A tear sparkled in her eyes, but it was not from sorrow. They dined leisurely, and when Marissa served the sweet honey cakes, the three agreed that this should be a regular gathering.

Later, Mark was just about to extinguish the lamp in his room when Benbusiris stepped to the door and asked if they could speak a bit more. He offered Mark a pouch of coins. By the weight of the offering, Mark was sure they were gold coins. "You have earned so much more than this. Will you take it?"

Mark shook his head. "Benbusiris, you are most generous, but I cannot take it. I tried to tell you that God's mercy cannot be purchased or sold. It has been God, working through prayer, that has finally moved Ianthe from darkness to light, from death to life. I'm happy for you, and for her. She is a delightful woman."

"Then what can I do to help her?" The father was frustrated in his helplessness.

"I have no experience to draw from, but I recall a young girl a few years ago that had a small lyre that she could play to lead us in singing. I think you should ask Ianthe first, but if you purchase a small music maker and perhaps find someone who can instruct her, it would be a happy day for Oriana and her grandfather."

As the lamps were extinguished Benbusiris was again amazed at the selfless depth of the man who was becoming far more than a guest in his house.

A Bold Beginning

The first request for a fellowship meeting came from the folks from the evening synagogue. They wanted to replace their attendance with a gathering led by Mark. He resisted, saying that the fellowship was for celebration. They continued to need the teaching from their Rabbi. When the morning group asked the same question, Mark sought permission from Benbusiris to host a group when Sabbath was over. He gave the invitation to both groups and was surprised when the crowd showed up. Nearly sixty folks filled the great room. They sang and prayed, and sang some more. Mark knew well the five points he wanted to share, but he kept the teaching brief, at least at first.

At the second meeting of the group they heard about God's Holy Spirit and the power to perform wondrous witness. He asked if anyone had an ailment, pain or disability. Three hands were raised and Mark asked them to come to the front. There, hands were laid upon them and a prayer for specific healing was given. As the final song was sung several in the group were already planning to bring others who needed this fellowship. Without articulating the fact, the Christian church had begun in Alexandria.

A Recovering Ianthe

Mark learned that the *Ianthe* was sailing to Joppa for a business meeting. He asked if it would be possible for him to accompany the ship to enable him to get to Jerusalem. He felt it necessary to tell James about the mission tour to Asia and Barnabas' death. He wasn't sure how much credit to take for the work that was only beginning in Alexandria. Surprisingly when the fellowship heard about Mark's plan to go to Jerusalem, they took a support offering to be presented to James. It was their way of declaring participation in a wonderful work. Then, when Benbusiris heard about their generosity, he added a great deal more to it. Now Mark had a double purpose there.

When Ianthe heard about the trip, however, her response was not so positive. She rose from the table and left the room. Both Benbusiris and Mark exchanged a worried look, and were silent for a tense moment. She came back in dabbing her tears.

"Please forgive me," she softly said. "I was shocked by the news, selfishly feeling the loss of something that is growing more and more precious to me." She looked at her father and then at Mark. "Your company at this table each night is what draws me through the day. I plan our conversations and think of jokes I can play on you. Forgive me for acting like a little girl."

Her father said, "We are just as fond of these meals. I vow that we will be gone less than two weeks." He looked at Mark for agreement.

The next day Marissa conveyed a private message to Benbusiris from his daughter. She wanted to talk with him alone.

"What can I do for you, Lamb?" a tender name he hadn't used in years.

"Abba, I want you to tell me the truth about Mark. Has he been so conscientious with me because you are paying him to do that?" Her gaze was direct.

"On my word, there is no conspiracy here," her father replied softly. "He has refused compensation for everything he has done for either you or me. I did manage to slip a few coins in the travelling bag, but I'm not sure how he is managing. Believe me, I did not ask him to do anything but pray for you." The father thought a moment and then added quietly, "And that was after I asked him to pray for me."

She said, "I don't understand how I feel about him. It feels on one hand that we are fresh new friends, but then on the other, it is like we are old, old friends. He seems to know my heart and has never abused that. I want to be with him all the time." She looked at the floor. "There are times at night when I hug my pillow and wish." She looked again into her father's eyes. "It would break my heart all over again if I learned that you have sent him on an Ianthe-rescue-mission."

"Sweet child, you must believe me; I am as fond of Mark as you are. In many ways he has filled the void of a lost son." It was as honest as any moment she could remember.

After shifting nervously, she asked quietly, "If I ask only him to dinner, will you understand that I simply need a bit of private conversation with him? I certainly don't want to offend you." A delicious smile slowly spread across her face. "I just need to give him the opportunity to tell me how much he cares for me. Yes, that might be devious, some might even call it manipulative, but I'm not getting any younger. I believe he just wants a little help, even though he doesn't know it."

They both chuckled, and the father marveled again at the transformation just eight months could bring, eight months and prayer.

Return to Jerusalem

In Joppa they agreed that it would take one day to get to Jerusalem, one more to meet with James, and one day back. They would sail south on the morning tide of the fourth day. To be a bit more protected, Benbusiris sent one of his men along with Mark as security. As the pair made their way through the busy street, few people paid any attention to Mark, but many saw the muscular man carrying a club with a Saracen knife at his waist.

Mark was sure he was in the right neighborhood, but it had been almost four years since he was last here. Then a small house looked familiar, without a gate or courtyard. He knocked on the doorsill. After a long pause an unfamiliar man opened the door and said nothing.

"I am John Mark, here to see James," He said politely.

The man reclosed the door and there was another long pause. Then the door was thrown open and the brother of Jesus stood before him wearing an enormous smile. "Mark come in this house! Who is your companion? Come in please!"

"Gill, the Egyptian, will be more comfortable watching the door." Mark responded. "I'm sure he would get nothing from our conversation, nor add anything to it. I have tried all day to get him to talk to me. He is my guardian." He revealed a heavy pouch of coins.

Once inside and seated at a small table, James said, "Tell me about your missions, after we pray." There followed a lengthy silence and then a heartfelt prayer of gratitude for a successful journey.

"The first part of our mission was wonderful," Mark began. "I had family business in Didyma, so we sailed there on a coastal freighter. Miletus was a disappointment, without a welcome or a moment of interest, so we hurried on to Ephesus, which was teeming with opportunity. With the hospitality of a couple tentmakers, we stayed for nine months and left a growing fellowship. There followed two years of struggling against either emperor worship or the influence of the Artemis priestesses. We visited Smyrna, Pergamum, Thyatira, Sardis, Philadelphia, and Laodicea. We tried to bless them with new understanding and spiritual grace. Barnabas was so wearied by the rejections he perceived, especially in Laodicea, that we stopped in Cyprus to renew our spirits."

Mark paused to catch his breath and quiet his emotions before he went on. "That's where the Pharisee's dagger man killed Uncle Barnabas." His listener gasped in shock. "A merchant who operates a coastal freighter rescued me from the melee. Ironically, we were not the assassin's targets, but Paul and Silas were. I have been in Alexandria for the past eight months. Here is a support offering that the new fellowship there and the merchant have sent to you." He placed the heavy pouch on the table, much to James' surprise. "There is also a very articulate young man named Apollos there, who is well trained in the scriptures and also sympathetic to the fellowship of Jesus. He seems interested in leadership."

"You have founded a fellowship in Egypt?" James asked astounded. "And you have done it alone after your partner was cut down?" He waited for a response.

Mark nodded his affirmation. "The merchant had overheard the plot to cut down a missionary named Paul and his companion," he replied. "The merchant is a righteous man and was at the forum to intervene if possible. It became obvious to him that he could only save one, and I was available. The knife that took Barnabas was intended for Paul and my father." The small room was silent until he added, "Gill, the Egyptian, is a deck hand for the merchant. Today he is once again responsible for my wellbeing."

"Would that all the followers had such security," James said heavily. "James, Andrew, and the Zealot Simon have all gone the way of Jesus. Now we must add the name of Barnabas to that list. Since Pilate was replaced, the Pharisees seem to be more bold in their attacks on the followers. Have you given consideration of where you will go next? Perhaps you can join Paul and your father. I believe they are in Corinth." James looked closely at Mark.

As the young man stood up, James noticed for the first time his fine linen tunic. He realized there had been a change in him, a handsome maturity. "James, I am grateful for your leadership here. I believe I need to spend time in prayer to find the Spirit's guidance. I will continue to lead the fellowship in Alexandria and perhaps recruit a new follower. I'll try to return in a few months. I'm sure there will be another support offering to help your work here. That may well be my best contribution of this effort."

James offered his hand, saying, "For one who was not an apostle, you have all the stature and spirit of one."

Outside, Mark said to Gill, "If we hurry we might be able to get some rest tonight in Lydda. That's three quarters of our way to Joppa. We might be on the morning tide tomorrow, a day early." He was thinking of a promise they had made to a lady with a haunting smile.

Benbusiris watched the two stride down the hill toward the harbor. He called to the crew to get ready to cast off. Somehow he understood the early arrival of the Jerusalem visitors as a sign of Mark's eagerness to return to a certain young lady. It made the father smile with satisfaction.

A Fresh Offer

On the second morning of their trip home, Benbusiris asked Mark, "Did they want to send you back on a mission?" He had waited for Mark to reveal the conversation and was too curious to let it rest any longer.

"The question was hinted," Mark said softly. "Apparently my father is in Corinth right now. James said I could join them. Frankly, I believe he was more impressed with our support gift. Things look pretty bare in Jerusalem, and by the sound of it there is growing Jewish opposition." The two men were quiet for a bit.

Mark sighed heavily and said, "There are many tangled thoughts in my head. I am very proud of the energy in our evening fellowship. Then at the same time I am drawn to the notion of becoming an innkeeper with a villa in Didyma." His eyes held those deep brown eyes of Benbusiris. "And above all there is Ianthe. I tried to tell myself my feelings for her were only compassion. She was in such a deep sorrow. I am a bit embarrassed to tell you that of late I can think of little else than the sound of her voice and her playful spirit. I'm happy she is nearly freed from her grief. But…" The gaze they shared did not blink.

Finally Benbusiris broke the silence, "But you are a marvelous young man with a healthy generous heart. I think I have an opportunity, you called it, that may not make the tangle any better. On the other hand it may be a solution." He had thought long on this and its ramifications. "Mark, I need someone I can greatly trust. I need someone who can do what I have been doing for the past five years; someone who can make contracts and then travel with the freight and collect the passage and make future contracts. There are many customers who count on us. It would be a demanding job, but a very lucrative one."

Mark realized the gruesome change that had happened five years ago that had shifted the responsibility from son back to father. "I think this conversation is going to rest for a while in prayer. Perhaps then the hand of the Lord will be more understandable." He finally looked down at his own folded hands, thinking he was eager to be home and receive a message from Ianthe.

When that occurred Mark was surprised. The invitation was for him only. Apparently she wanted to speak to him alone. Mark changed into a fresh tunic.

Marissa had prepared boiled fish with a melon and very fresh bread. The food, however, was secondary to both the diners. Mark enjoyed simply studying Ianthe's face and listening to the gentleness of her voice. Ianthe was distracted by her feelings when his eyes were so intent upon her. It had been too long since she had felt that warmth.

After a very long silence, she said, "I wished to thank you for the wonder of a healed heart. I have no idea how, or much more why, you managed to bring me back to life. I think I knew that you are a very special man when you made the toy for Oriana. She never knew her father, so it was my grief that had swallowed us both. When I saw her laugh and play with you, I knew she was leading me out of the cloud of tears. Your prayers assured me that life could proceed." Her hand reached across the corner of the table toward Mark's hand. "I want to touch you, perhaps hold you. I feel full of hope today." Her gray eyes studied his face.

As he wrapped his hand around hers he spoke in a playful way, "I hurried us home because I so missed you. Your father tried to explore my future, and I confessed a strong confusion. The one thing I am sure of is that I want to be near you often."

"How near," she quietly asked, "and how often?" The smile that danced across her face was a silent love song that they both recognized and welcomed.

Shyly he answered, "I can only tell you that everything about this moment feels right. My heart is urging me to tell you of my affection for you, which seems to grow deeper and dearer each day. I think you already know that. When I know the path of my future I will ask you to share it with me." He really did not want to release her soft hand. But he did.

She reclasped his hand and said with obvious longing, "My heart is still healing, but it already knows it wants to follow you on whatever path you choose. May I attend the fellowship with you?"

"Yes, of course! That would be wonderful! If I tell your father that you will be there, I'm pretty sure he will join with us too. Nothing could make me happier." As she released his hand, Mark added, "Your father has invited me officially to become part of the shipping industry. I think my only choice is between an Inn in Didyma, or a happy life here in Alexandria. It feels to me as though the choice is made."

Fellowship Success

On the first day of the week at sunset, the fellowship gathered. There must have been eighty gathered in Benbusiris' home and an additional twenty standing in the courtyard. Mark positioned himself where both parts could hear. They sang, and he prayed, and they sang again. The theme of the evening was forgiveness, so many selections from the prophets dealt with the sure judgment of God.

Mark said, "I remember a teaching story that Peter told on himself. He asked Jesus, 'Lord how many times shall I forgive my brother when he sins against me? Up to seven times?' I imagine Peter thought he was being generous for the Law says we ought to forgive three times."

"Jesus answered, 'I tell you not seven times, but seventy times seven times.

"'Therefore the kingdom of heaven is like a king who wanted to settle accounts with his servants. As he began the settlement, a man who owed him ten thousand talents was brought to him. Since he was not able to pay, the master ordered that he and his wife and his children and all that he had be sold to repay the debt.'

"The servant fell on his knees before the king. 'Be patient with me,' he begged, 'and I will pay back everything.' The servant's master took pity on him, cancelled the debt and let him go.' Some folks snickered in disbelief.

"But when that servant went out, he found one of his fellow servants who owed him a hundred denarii. He grabbed him and began to choke him. 'Pay back what you owe me! he demanded.'

"'His fellow servant fell on his knees and begged him, 'Be patient with me, and I will pay you back.'

"'But he refused. Instead he went off and had the man thrown into prison until he could pay the debt. When the other servants saw what happened they were greatly distressed and went and told their master everything that had happened.'

"'Then the master called the servant in. 'You wicked servant,' he said, 'I cancelled all that debt of yours because you begged me to. Shouldn't you have had mercy on your fellow servant just as I had on you?' In anger the master turned him over to the jailers to be tortured, until he should pay back all he owed.'

"'This is how my heavenly Father will treat each of you unless you forgive your brother from your heart.'"

Mark was certain the story had introduced many new concepts to the listeners. He explained the story with the conclusion that all of them have unforgiven sins. "Why wait another moment if forgiveness is here before you? There is no such thing as a little sin if it stands between you and God. God is pleading for you to ask for forgiveness." He taught them the prayer Jesus had taught that they could say all together, called the Believer's prayer. One of the petitions asked, "forgive us our sins as we forgive those who sin against us."

He led the group in the singing of another song, and he prayed a prayer. Finally he said, "If you sincerely asked, God has sincerely forgiven you! May the powerful peace of God keep your hearts this night and always." Several people wanted to speak with him more, but none as much as Benbusiris and his daughter.

At the Same Time in Didyma

Six men and a woman, soiled by travel and neglect, waited on the dock. They were guarded by four grouchy looking Roman soldiers, who had bound their hands behind their back; a rope noose around their neck warned any bystander to stand clear or join them. They had been in Corinth, trying to share the story of Jesus' love and mercy, his great sacrifice and victory. Jews that had gotten both Paul and Silas beaten once in Philippi (Acts 16:22) had been following Paul from town to town. Their intent was assassination, but again they had missed him, so they settled for these followers of the one called Christ Jesus.

They whipped the crowd into a frenzy with unsubstantiated accusations. Some bullies on one side of the crowd had started a fight, and those on the other side started two fires. The authorities came in to restore peace and grabbed these accused radicals. When they learned that one still had the welts and bruises from a previous beating, they had all the evidence they needed. They got a magistrate to pass judgment, and the seven rioters were condemned to prison until they could satisfy the debt, which rarely happened. They were marched to Didyma and scheduled for exile in the prison dungeon on Patmos.

The woman whispered to the man tied in front of her, "Silas, what will become of us?"

Outstanding Response

The fellowship grew each week. Mark sought Benbusiris' permission to add another evening, and then a third. The young man named Apollos asked if he could lead another. Soon there was a fellowship meeting every night of the week somewhere in the city, and no one seemed to object.

During that time Mark was praying that God might show him how to bring healing to Benbusiris. Mark helped him see the advantage of making the navigator of each boat a second in command that would take care of rescheduling contracts for future ship assignments, which replaced the need for an administrator to be aboard. It also seemed to Mark that having the freight prepaid would be practical. He had said, "Why should you take on all the liability. If pirates attack or a terrible storm sets in, you may lose the ship; that's your responsibility. If the cargo is lost that is not on you."

Mark began a conscientious calendar, making a more efficient use of ships while minimizing their return to port empty. He kept books on costs and profits, lists of crewmen and wages to be paid. He cut costs and increased profits. And he did all that without having to leave port. Or said another way, he did that and still was able to eat the evening meal with Benbusiris and his daughter. The father was delighted. Mark realized that his prayers were being answered. Without telling anyone, it was obvious that Benbusiris was releasing the bitterness of grief just as his daughter had.

One quiet Sabbath they were seated at the table. Oriana was strumming her lyre, now rather proficiently. Benbusiris wore a huge smile of satisfaction. "Mark," the senior man began, "I am having a very strange problem."

"How may I help you?" Mark said with a concerned expression.

"You have been with us for more than two years and have accepted no compensation other than a few coins I have been able to sneak into your travelling bag. I'll wager you have even given those tiny morsels to the poor. Don't you think it is overtime to make a decision about the Didyma Inn?" The look on his face was something between anguish and pleading.

"Benbusiris, sir, I live in a palace, eat like a lord and have the use of this home for fellowships. That is enormous compensation. I have been able to do God's will, and I can't ask for any more. But you are correct, sir. There are large decisions to be made. I must get to Didyma to conclude my affairs there. Do you suppose I may find passage on one of your ships?"

Both the father and daughter had major smiles on their faces. They now were confident that Mark had chosen to make this his home, however that might be worked out.

"Yes, we can do that. This is a calm season on the Great Sea. If *Ianthe* sails due north, we will be there in six days." He looked at his daughter and assured her, "We will return before the change of the month."

Mark wanted to argue for a more modest plan, until Ianthe said softly, "That will put my worst fears to rest." The decision was made.

Ten days later Mark recognized the point that opened to the Didyma harbor. He knew that the decisions about to be made would forever change his life, but he was unaware of the dramatic scope of those changes. He was eager for Benbusiris to see the inn and the villa above it.

When they trudged up the hill the Inn seemed somewhat smaller than Mark remembered. Once he walked through the door, he knew there had been a change. There were a couple dozen officers at the tables. The atmosphere seemed labored, and the young innkeeper who came out to greet him didn't recognize him. "I'm seeking the innkeeper Luscious," Mark said warmly.

"You are about a year too late," the innkeeper said with a serious expression. "My father died suddenly. I am Martain, his son."

Mark said, "I am John Mark, son of Silvanus of Jerusalem." He noticed a Roman look up from his meal to study him.

"Do you have proof of that?" Martain asked, still guarded.

Mark leaned over and made a sigma in the dust of the floor. He turned and made another across it.

Martain asked, "What can I do for you, sir?

"We would welcome a bowl of the stew, and a cup of wine. Then I would like to see the ledger your father kept for me." There was no demand, just a pleasant request. The Roman continued to study the activity at their table.

The stew, a plate of bread and figs, and a cup of cool wine was served immediately. The account didn't appear until they had finished eating. Martain explained, "Father's first entry was almost twenty years ago. For the past five years he has been more detailed. But I think you will find the current balances."

The first six years were deposits that grew to an impressive balance. Then three times a year there were sizable expenditures as well as a few deposits. Seven years ago the expenditures were two a year, still with regular deposits. Five years ago there was a large deposit and a sizable expenditure as well as the two regular expenditures. The current balance for JM showed forty three thousand denarii; the balance for S showed seventeen thousand. For the past four years the deposits had been modestly uniform, and the two expenditures remained large.

"Can you explain these balances for me?" Mark asked.

The Roman stood up and approached their table. He was an impressive man who wore his uniform with dignity and spoke to others without their permission. "Did I hear you say that you are the son of Silvanus?" he asked Mark.

"Yes, that's my father's name," Mark answered trying hard not to be intimidated.

"Was he the Tribute Consul for the prefect of Judea?" he pressed.

"Yes, that was my father's privilege," Mark replied. "How can I be of service to a Centurion?"

"It might be what service I can be to you. Twenty years ago I was a security officer that traveled the territory with him, gathering taxes. I remember him as an honorable citizen and a completely honest man."

"Indeed he is," Mark wondered where this journey through the past was going.

The Centurion gave a soft chuckle and said, "As an honest man, he managed the most entertaining deception I have ever imagined." The word ran a cold shiver down Mark's spine. "Prefect Pilate wanted a prison built for greater control over the people. Your father told him that he would build a death dungeon with private funds, if the governor would simply dedicate a remote island for it. It was truly a masterful joke on a despot governor. For the last twenty years your father has sent lumber for homes and food for the people. Only Jews have been sent there, since Greeks are sentenced to real prisons. He has rescued hundreds of victims from Jewish justice." His final words were chilling. "Ironically, a year ago he was part of a group of rioters sentenced to exile on Patmos." He reached out his hand to shake Mark's. "For a silver coin you may liberate him, if he wants to leave his captive haven. There are no locked doors or cells, just three old gatekeepers who watch the flock." He turned and walked out leaving Mark to ponder the impact of his words.

Martain had listened to the Centurion's account; then turning to the books, he said, "For ten years there was a lumber shipment annually and two food shipments to the island. For the past ten years it has been two shipments of food. They have received goats and sheep, fruit trees and garden seeds. I believe it was your father's plan to have the island self-sufficient when the funds ran out. As you can see, that time is near." The two sons held a gaze.

Martain continued, "I am glad you are here for another reason. Our fathers had an agreement, which I believe is well satisfied. I have a home in Caesarea, a family, and a job as a ship's navigator when I am needed. I am not much of an innkeeper. My family is living in the villa while I am here; it has felt quite temporary. I have found buyers for both the inn and the villa, which are the final two holdings of your father. It has been my plan to sell them and let the funds run out on supplies for the island. Now you can make that decision more responsibly." Benbusiris was listening to the conversation with interest, and Mark was pondering how this might fit into the Centurion's news.

"I believe," Mark said finally, "my first obligation is to go to Patmos and offer my father his freedom. Then the future of all this will be made clear." Looking at Benbusiris he asked, "Can *Ianthe* negotiate the eight miles?"

"Of course, if we have a navigator." He was smiling for the day had brought him another possibility, and there was yet enough daylight to make the trip out and back. Martain said it would be his honor to guide them there.

A Happy Rescue Mission

The interested Roman soldier watched the sleek ship maneuver to the island dock. It was obvious more prisoners were not aboard, nor supplies. He stood at the top of the ramp waiting for information.

"Yes, I am familiar with the one called Silas, and those who were sentenced with him." He was aware that the young man asking held a pouch of coins. "If you go to the third row of houses and turn left toward the hill, someone will guide you to him."

Benbusiris went with Mark, more out of curiosity than security. They asked two people before the house was pointed out. Mark was trembling as he knocked on the side of the house. It had been almost six years since he had seen his father. A woman's face appeared at the door and Mark asked if this was the house of Silas. The father's curious face transformed into joy the moment he recognized his son. Benbusiris who was closely watching the exchange also released a sigh of relief.

"How did you find me?" Silas asked, "and how did you get here?" His embrace tried to bridge the ones lost over time.

"Father this is Benbusiris, who saved my life in Paphos and has become a beacon of support. It was his charity that prevented the assassin's knife from taking my life as well as Uncle Barnabas'." A shocked frown clouded the father's face at the terrible announcement of his brother-in-law's death. "He owns a shipping line and brought me here from Alexandria to release you. The Centurion at the inn told us how to find you. He was not sure you would want to be released from this, your most secret ruse." The son didn't want to release his embrace.

"I must hear more about the Pathos matter," Silas said as he reached behind himself to present the woman to Mark. "This is Sharon. Her husband was a Roman soldier who was killed in battle. With no family she received a bit of a pension, but has needed our support since it stopped. She has been a great help with the fellowships." Then speaking more softly he added, "She also treated the infections on my back. The second flogging was on top of the unhealed first one. I needed her care and she needed my sheltering. Our relationship was born out of necessity but has bloomed into devotion. We pledged our fidelity in prayer and received the blessings of those with us."

It was obvious that Silas was trying to comprehend the many levels of information in the moment. "You say that you are here to free me? There were five others with us." Mark noted the inclusion of Sharon. "Is it possible to bring them too?" Silas looked around waving his hand. "This isn't bad for a prison, but I'm sure they would all agree that we would like to be somewhere else." He still had a rich sense of leadership and humor.

Benbusiris shook another coin pouch, saying, "Bring whomever you choose. I imagine there won't be much baggage. We still have enough light to be back in Didyma by sunset." He even gave the gatekeeper soldier an extra silver coin as they all climbed back aboard *Ianthe*.

Five of the freed men chose to continue on the road home rather than stop at the inn. After freshening a bit, and dining on a bowl of lamb stew, bread and a cup of wine, Silas said with obvious satisfaction, "It has been more than a year. This was an elegant meal. All that you have done to make this possible is wonderful." There were tears in his eyes.

"Father, I believe God's hand has been at work here," Mark said firmly. "We came to Didyma to inspect the inn. I have wondered if this is my destiny. Should I be an innkeeper? There is another road for me to follow in Alexandria. In the last year we have started more and stronger fellowships than any on the missionary trail. At the same time I have learned a great deal about shipping. I find your presence here an answer to several prayers. It is your inn to do with as you wish, and just up the hill is a very comfortable villa, which you own as well. The ledger is here to show you still have enough in the account to get a very nice fresh start. This could become a perfect location for hospitality and fellowship."

The smile on Benbusiris' face hadn't faded since this conversation began. It was about to grow even larger as Mark said, "Father, there is a young widow in Alexandria who has won my heart completely. When I can earn a bride's-price to offer her father, I will seek his blessing to become her husband. It may be that I am now in the presence of both my father and my future father in law." Benbusiris embraced Mark like never before.

"Yes, you may have her hand in marriage," he said gleefully, even though Mark had not officially asked. Then he embraced Silas and Sharon as well.

A Wonderfully Serious Relationship

True to their promise, before the new month Mark and Benbusiris were at the table with Ianthe and Oriana. Benbusiris was giving an account of their adventure with special emphasis on the accomplishments of Mark's father.

Ianthe asked in surprise, "You mean to say that he lied to the Roman Prefect?"

Benbusiris nearly giggled, "He didn't lie. He asked for the dedication of an island for the establishment of a dungeon of punishment, which would be constructed with private funds. He did mislead the governor into thinking it would be a dreadful punishment when in fact it was quite acceptable. The great irony is that Patmos became a shelter for the very one who had dreamed it up in the first place." His obvious enjoyment of the entire hoax was shared by the others.

After a lengthy silence, Ianthe asked "Abba, may I ask you an awkward question?" Her expression didn't give him any indication of concern.

Mark asked if it would be appropriate for him to leave the table.

"Oh no," Ianthe smiled, "It sort of involves you as well." She peered at her father, and then said softly, "It has been seven years since Mathias' death. Oriana doesn't know what it's like to have others in the house. Would it be a great inconvenience if I sell this house and move back in with you? We are eating together regularly anyway. It would give her a sense of family." Her innocent smile warned the father there might be more to the plan than was being voiced.

He replied, "I was about to ask you the same question since I am more and more fatigued by the walk over here every evening. It would be far more convenient if you were back in your old room."

His expression, while guarded, let her understand she had not fooled him, but perhaps Mark had missed the meaning of the exchange.

Innocently he said, "I think it is past due for me to find my own housing. I have been too long a guest in your home." Both the other two chuckled and nodded agreement, to his shock.

Benbusiris said, "We have been trying to allow you freedom to come to this conclusion by yourself. Since that hasn't happened, let me act as the match-maker and give you a tiny assistance. Mark, you haven't been a guest for the past two years. You are a beloved part of us. We are simply looking for a way to make it obvious for you. My house is grossly too large for one old man. But it is plenty spacious for a family. Don't you think it is time for you to find a loving wife? You cannot forever be a homeless missionary. When will you settle down?" The senior man looked him in the eyes and said bluntly, "I want more grandchildren. Oriana wants a father's affection, and Ianthe wants someone to warm her bed. I do believe that God wants you to join with her in marriage."

Mark asked in a soft voice, "Ianthe, is that true."

"Well my list has a bit more on it than the warm bed part, but it a great place to begin. Yes, it is all true."

"You both must know how honored and humbled I am" Mark said with his boyish grin. "Of course I have dreamed of this, but it seemed unattainable." He mumbled something about being at a lack of the appropriate words. Then he said simply, "It seems to me the only thing lacking here is a proposal." He reached for Ianthe's hand. "I have only held this hand once before, even though I wanted to so often. Your father has blessed us. With all my heart I do believe that God has brought us to this moment with his divine will." He took a deep breath and asked softly, "Ianthe, will you be my wife? Will we remain together for as long as we have breath?" There were tears in their eyes.

"In the presence of Abba and the God of Abraham, I am honored and humbled to be asked and to be able to say, 'Yes, I will gladly be your wife, finally.'"

Benbusiris came around the table to embrace his daughter first, and then included Mark. "Two years ago this was simply a wonderful fantasy," he said. "I had no idea we could ever be this happy again. Thanks be unto God, and, Mark, thanks be to you."

A Wedding!

Rabbi Benjamin from the Sabbath Eve synagogue was pleased to be asked to conduct the wedding. It gave him assurance that the large group from his congregation were still loyal to it. It also showed him the faithful side of the evening fellowship that gathered in celebration. The questions he asked led several to wonder if the rabbi might be interested in regular attendance with them as well.

In some ways the change in marital status was hardly evident. Mark still arose early each day to be in prayer and after a light meal, he was ready for work in the shipping office. He was home promptly in the evening, eager for dinner with Benbusiris, Ianthe and Oriana. His life was wonderfully predictable.

In other ways the change was profound. He awoke each morning next to a lovely wonder. Her affection was honest and very welcome. The entire family was always present at the table for breakfast, which was preceded by songs and prayer. Oriana demonstrated a sweet young voice that would one day be widely recognized. She also appreciated the hug from Mark that signaled the affection of a father she was growing to love more each day. Benbusiris radiated joy in his happy home, which rarely gave evidence of the previous sorrow that had stifled it.

Gentle days pass slowly, but accumulate surprisingly. Suddenly four Sabbaths have gone past and it was a new month, and then another. One of the sure ways to create a new agenda was in Ianthe's announcement that she was pregnant! That brought everything to a new focus. Perhaps Oriana cried the most; she was ecstatic to become a big sister. It was a balance between Mark and Benbusiris. They were both thrilled.

In the bedroom darkness one night Ianthe asked Mark if he was still awake. "I am so filled with joy I am having trouble getting to sleep," she told him.

"May I rub your back?" her husband whispered. "That seems to be a relaxing moment for you."

"Mark, I am so very grateful for you. I can scarcely remember the dark days of grief and despair. Now your touch thrills me, and I have a new being within me. I think this is the abundant life. Are you as happy as I am?"

He laughed softly, saying, "I don't think either of us is as happy as your father. Did you see him after your announcement? He was like the rooster who gets to awaken the sun each morning. Yes, I am extremely happy for all of us."

She wiggled a bit tighter against him. "What would make you happier?" she asked a bit playfully.

After a bit of reflection, Mark answered innocently, "Your well being and the baby's are my greatest concerns. I pray for a healthy birth. Beyond that, perhaps eventually I would like to visit my father." He knew it would be easy for their conversation to turn to something far more stimulating, which seemed to be her intent.

Ianthe followed his mood. "Are you wishing for a son or a daughter?"

"I can think of equal delight in either one," her tactful husband answered. "Have you thought about names?" He was distracted by the warmth of her body pressed against him.

"I think that should be your task," she replied. "But my favorite boy's name has been Gabriel, which means the 'man of God.'" Her voice broke with a stifled laugh. "For a girl a fine name would be Gloria, a word for 'praise.' But it is really up to you." She giggled into the covers and wiggled even closer. She wasn't a bit sleepy.

Attended by two midwives, Gabriel was born on a pleasant spring morning. Eight year old Oriana had a healthy baby brother. When she was ten, she had another one named Michael, which means 'Who is like the Lord?' And when she was twelve, she finally had a baby sister named Gloria.

During that time Mark was a diligent student, learning about the shipping industry. As Benbusiris' assistant, he watched, listened and learned. He was attentive at problem solving and frequently found a more efficient answer to office problems. He was not a ruthless negotiator, but usually came up with a fair solution there too. All the while the fellowships continued to thrive. It had become common practice for them to outgrow whatever space they were using, so a division would occur to make more availability. There were more than thirty meetings happening across the city each week. Mark had made an annual trip to Jerusalem to deliver support to those who were still there. He also managed to visit his father once a year.

Sorrow

Benbusiris enjoyed seven more years of doting over his large family. If there was a more proud grandfather in Alexandria, he must have been living in the rural part, because Benbusiris explained to business contacts, fellowship attendees, and even strangers on the street what wonderful grandchildren he had. One morning he came to the breakfast table complaining that he was in some discomfort. His eye was teary and the corner of his mouth was drooping. As he talked, his speech became slurred and difficult to understand. Ianthe suggested he should lie down for a bit to see if his discomfort would ease. When she went into check on him a few minutes later he was unresponsive. She ran for Mark. When they hurried in, they found the patriarch was not breathing and listening to his chest, there was no heartbeat. Gabriel was asked to run to Rabbi Benjamin's with the alarming news. In only a few minutes the rabbi came, accompanied by the local judge. They determined that indeed he had died of heart failure.

Ianthe produced a letter her father had given her in the event of his death. It mainly transferred all property holdings to Mark and his heirs. It had instructions for contacting his investments and special consideration for several long-time employees. The final paragraph stipulated that he did not want to have his body buried in the ground or burned on a pier, but rather immediately buried at sea.

It only took Mark until the third hour to arrange the crew, transfer the body, and prepare *Ianthe* for a short cruise. Ianthe decided the sea burial was not an image she wanted for herself or her children. They would wait for Mark at home. As it turned out, it was an important morning. He was not the captain; now he gave the captain orders and the crew understood the shift. After sailing north for about an hour, he asked the captain to lower the sails. He went to the windward side, positioned Benbusiris' shroud-covered body, and invited the crew to gather. Hats were removed in respect, and the men quietly listened to a prayer and then words of committal to the deep. The weighted body slid out from under a sheet and gently sank as the ship drifted away from the site. It was a reverent moment filled with honor, both for Benbusiris and for Mark, the new boss, who asked the captain to hoist the sails and return to port.

It was not a perfectly smooth transition of leadership. Benbusiris had, however arranged details well enough for it to be an efficient one. The only omission was Mark's annual trip to Didyma, as there just wasn't an opportunity for that. Two years passed quickly before he could reunite with his father and Sharon. The news he heard then was gravely distressing. James had been stoned to death in Jerusalem, and Paul was in prison in Rome.

Silas said, "Paul has requested your assistance there in Rome. I do believe he would like you to write letters and record pages for him, even though the Macedonian physician seems to be doing that satisfactorily."

Mark told his father, "Sadly the shipping demands will not permit me to consider that."

Then Silas reported that several church fellowships were faltering, but many, like Antioch, Ephesus, Thessalonica, and Corinth were dynamic in their witness. Aquila and Priscilla had returned to Rome with a thriving church in their home.

Silas confided that he and Sharon were enjoying the life of ease. The inn served one meal a day on a subscription plan to the Roman officers. Their waiting list became long enough to offer a later seating. Now they served about a hundred a night, many of them former security people who had accompanied him. "There is ample income with little effort on our part. We have five people doing the cooking and serving and cleanup, which allows us to spend time in our gracious courtyard. I get to socialize and maintain a cordial atmosphere at the inn. We are quite content as we grow older." His chuckle was welcome and comforting for a son who lived far from his father.

In the following three years Mark had such demand for shipping he ordered another large freighter and another coastal cruiser, which he named *Oriana*. Both were brought into service as quickly as possible and booked regularly.

Parenting Lesson

One afternoon Mark was making his way home; it had been a trying day. While he was still a distance from the house, he heard a child's piercing scream. It caused him to break into a lope to investigate. Before he could get to the gate he heard yet another scream followed by a sob. He burst into the house to find Gabriel standing over Gloria; he was making a hideous growl.

"Gabriel, stop that!" he commanded as he rushed between the children. Gloria jumped up and grasped the protective leg, trembling. "What are you thinking?" he barked at the still grinning boy.

"We are playing dragons," the lad answered, still in the mood of the game. "It's fun."

"Does it look to you like your sister is enjoying the game?" The tone of his voice signaled the boy that there might not be agreement.

Gabriel noticed tears running down his little sister's cheeks. "No, sir," he answered softly. "She doesn't like it at all."

"Where is Oriana?" Mark asked heatedly.

The fun was over, and the son realized he was being addressed for correction. "She and mother went to the marketplace to find some fabrics."

"It was your responsibility as the older to care for Gloria, not torment her." An idea was forming to teach a lesson. "But since you are so brave, I have a chore for you tomorrow. The bilge of *Lunar Ox* is being pumped out. I need someone brave enough to carry a bucket of smoldering hemp through the bilge to smoke out the rats. There are two or three that are large enough to attack a man. Perhaps your dragon's roar might keep you safe. Just wear a loin cloth under your tunic because it is quite filthy down there." The son shuddered at the prospect that he knew was not an option.

Years later he would confide with his father that the chore was the vilest test he had ever endured. "It was dark and foul down there. The sting of smoke in my eyes and lungs was unavoidable. My throat hurt from trying to growl like a beast. I saw many rats on their way off the ship, but none as large as you described. Then I realized you had allowed me to feel the anxiety I had given Gloria. Only when it was over and I was cleansed could I understand the lesson. I've never forgotten that every choice we make has a consequence. The art is in choosing wisely and not carelessly."

The episode also stuck with the father. Its recollection of the horrific scourge of dragons would serve him in completing the last major task of his life.

Shifting Political Wind

The Roman garrison commander approached Mark for an urgent trip to Miletus. He and two other officers had to get there as quickly as possible. They strongly suggested that *Oriana* be ready to leave at dawn. They would be returning after a very brief military orientation. The only good part of their demand was they prepaid without hesitation. Mark accompanied the trip as their steward, taking advantage of the lay-over as a brief visit with his father.

He was careful not to obviously eavesdrop, but there seemed to be little concern over what conversations he did hear. Apparently there was a major buildup of Roman troops from the north. Some action was being planned against Jerusalem, of all places. On the morning they arrived at Didyma, Mark was told that the Roman plan involved cutting off any southern escape from Jerusalem. The officer said, "Be careful what you carry. From now on Joppa or Caesarea are restricted ports. If you transport in supplies or rescue fleeing Hebrews, we will necessarily see it as an act of treason. The results will be most unpleasant for you and your fleet."

As the Commander left the vessel, he said, "You have this day to replenish stores. We especially liked the boiled shrimp and the fresh bread. Your accommodations have been appreciated." It was close enough to a compliment coming from a Roman officer.

The inn was empty except for the cook who recognized the owner's son. He agreed that he could purchase the needed stores and have them delivered to the ship. "That will give you an hour or two with your father," he said softly. "He has expressed great pride in you, and a keen sorrow you are so far apart." A small pouch of gold coins exchanged hands, ensuring that the task of fresh stores would be accomplished.

When Mark found his father and Sharon at the villa, he was surprised at how gray their hair was becoming. After lengthy embraces, Mark explained the cause of this unexpected visit. "The commander was not hostile to me, but he warned against taking on passengers from Joppa or Caesarea who might be fleeing from something."

His father nodded, "I received a similar warning from several officers. They cautioned me away from any crowd gatherings that might appear hostile to the Romans. There is a confrontation coming that must be very large. Troops are coming from the north in large numbers. There is an army of might gathering in Miletus. The good side of that is a growing number of officers to feed." He reminded his son how irrational people in power can be. "We were accused of rioting when it was the temple guards crashing in our door."

Sharon wanted to be part of the conversation. "We were giving our witness when we were arrested for rioting, and sent to Patmos." She smiled warmly and finished the thought, "There are few prisons as nice as that one." Her arm slid around Silas.

"I hope you know," Mark said affectionately, "you are always welcome to come to Alexandria. If it becomes dangerous here for you, there are many ships bound for Egypt.

"Oh my," his father chuckled, "we are too old to move again. I really do like it here. We may need to add another serving time for more officers, but they are cordial and appreciative of good food and wine, and pay well. I'm not sure we feel safe, but we do not fear our Roman friends. It is nice, however, for you to express concern for us."

"Mark, there has been much sad news," he continued. "It seems that Paul has been executed, as has Peter. I'm afraid the only Apostle still living is John, son of Zebedee. I was told he is staying in Ephesus. The Jews are still a much graver threat to our movement than the Romans."

Mark was quick to say, "That's another reason why you might want to visit Alexandria. There must be nearly fifty evening fellowships, and

I have heard of no resentment about any of them. We have three meeting in our home each week."

"With different folks attending?" his father asked with surprise.

"Oh, yes. We have room for about a hundred each evening." Then Mark gave a proud father's account of the grandchildren's uniqueness. He concluded with, "Ianthe is a proud wife and mother, and a very devoted follower of Jesus. My life is a song of joy."

They chatted through the afternoon, shared a light meal together and prayed. Mark acknowledged that he had to get back to the *Oriana*. They must be prepared to leave at dawn. A person never understands until later how precious last moments are.

The crew was at their stations as they watched the three Roman officers descend the hill. Once they were on board Mark informed them that the wind had shifted from the north, a distinct advantage and their journey home would be calm and a day shorter.

Back in Alexandria, as the Commander was leaving the ship he shook Mark's hand and complimented him on the exceptional service. "Your ship has served us well. By land that journey would have taken more than a weary month one way. You made the round trip in a comfortable eleven days. My men are aware of your protected status in the conflict that is approaching. Please don't do anything that would cause me to regret that."

That ominous warning was verified within the year when two small competitors took material into Joppa. Their ships were destroyed and the supplies confiscated. The rest of their fleet at the dock in Alexandria was also burned to the waterline and sunk. Something very terrible was beginning.

Historians would call it the Jewish Revolt; others saw it as a very one-sided battle. Rome put a siege around Jerusalem, the Holy city. Those who tried to escape were killed. Those who tried to stay were eventually starved. Perhaps initially, the story of the successful battle of the Maccabees, four hundred years before, rang out a hope for freedom from the Roman occupation. But the might of Rome could not be compared to an Assyrian army. In the end Jerusalem was completely destroyed; tens of thousands were slain.

As hard as that was to believe there was an additional tragedy. The center district of Rome caught fire and the conflagration, which burned for several days, was blamed on the Christians. There were some who believed Nero needed an urban renewal project, and the Christians were merely convenient scapegoats. In either case the beginning of a ruthless persecution of Christians was wide-spread and unrelenting, reaching its most intense brutality in the reign of Emperor Domitian.

Many Years Later

Mark studied the lovely wrinkles he had been privileged to appreciate for more than thirty years. Their bodies had grown old and unsteady, but their eyes still held the warmth of affection. Their lovely home was quiet these days. Oriana had married one of the ship captains. Gabriel was the acting fleet manager, with a wife and family. Michael was busy building fellowships in the thirty three major cities north of Alexandria and Gloria had married a wine merchant. Now in retirement Mark's principle concern was his powerlessness to help the churches decimated by the persecution. "Perhaps I can take them a support offering to show my concern."

Ianthe answered softly, "Perhaps," then as an after-thought, she said, "I understand collaborators are being arrested as well. You would be little help to anyone from a cell, or worse, a cross."

"But doing nothing seems such a poor witness," he mused.

She looked at his face for a silent moment. So long ago when she had seen him for the first time, even through the tears of her grief, she had thought him a strikingly handsome man. She still felt that way and a tiny tremble passed through her. "Mark is there anything you regret today?" she asked tenderly.

He rubbed the side of his face as he thought about an answer. She loved it when he exhibited that mannerism. Finally he said, "My only regret is that I failed to complete the scroll manuscript, even when Matthew and others so urged me to do it. That resurrection finish would have been very important for the faith of the readers."

Ianthe had a sparkle in her eyes as she said, "Can you imagine an epistle that would circulate among the churches, speaking now to a hopeless people, telling them of a certain victory, that the forces of God cannot be denied?" When he pursed his mouth, about to say,

"No," she added, "I remember when I thought I was beaten by grief. You told me that portion of my life was over, but I would get more. Do you remember that? I began to get stronger simply by holding onto that promise."

"If I should write anything that may be understood as politically inflammatory, our entire family could be punished," Mark whispered.

"Then write something mystical or magical that would appear as a children's fantasy, something about stars with angels and dragons or mythical beasts. Your father did a wonderful thing right in front of the prefect's eyes. You could do something similar. Write something that would be nonsense to an unbeliever, but encouraging to the eyes of faith."

For a moment Mark was bathed in a wave of affection for this woman who seemed to understand his very soul. After a long thoughtful silence, however, he said wearily, "I don't know what I'm thinking. How could I have anything relevant to say in such a perilous time?"

"I will never understand men," Ianthe murmured to herself. "They never seem to learn from their mistakes." Looking steadily into her husband's eyes, she said, "You regret not writing the resurrection account, finishing your scroll. A few years from now how will you feel about not writing something that could stem the tide of destructive hopelessness?"

"But my style is recognizable. I could cause havoc for our family and the shipping company," he said in a small voice. "I have honed my craft too well not to be recognized."

"Then leave it unwritten if you choose" she sighed. "I will not try to urge you further. But a smart man could forget the proper rules and pen a crude epistle that would carry more interest. But it is up to you. I won't mention it again."

In the darkness he listened to her slow breathing and knew that she was correct. The churches needed his assistance and he could do it. Visions of inspiration began to collect in his imagination and again he remembered the final words of Barnabas, "Jesus is Lord!"

After a Sleepless Night

In the morning he took a sheet of papyrus and began a new scroll:

"The revelation of Jesus Christ, which God gave him to show us his servants what must soon take place; and he made it known by sending his angel to his servant John, who bore witness to the word of God and to the testimony of Jesus Christ, even to all that he saw. Blessed is he who reads aloud the words of the prophecy, and blessed are those who hear, and who keep what is written therein; for the time is near.

John to the seven churches that are in Asia:

Grace to you and peace from him who is and who was and who is to come, and from the seven spirits who are before his throne, and from Jesus Christ the faithful witness, the first born of the dead, and the ruler of kings on earth.

To him who loves us and freed us from our sins by his blood and made us a kingdom, priests to his God and Father, to him be glory and dominion for ever and ever. Amen.

"I am the Alpha and the Omega," says the Lord God, who is and who was and who is to come, the Almighty.

I John, your brother, who share with you in Jesus the tribulation and the kingdom and the patient endurance, was on the island called Patmos on account of the word of God and the testimony of Jesus. I was in the Spirit on the Lord's Day, and I heard behind me a loud voice like a trumpet saying, 'Write what you see in a book and send it to the seven churches, to Ephesus and to Smyrna and to Pergamum and to Thyatira and to Sardis and to Philadelphia and to Laodicea.

Then I turned to see the voice that was speaking to me, and on turning I saw seven golden lamp stands ...." (The Revelation to John ff)

Confirmation Class Finale

Confirmation Sunday was always a special time. At the end of the service, the class was presented; they answered the usual questions and then read their chosen Bible verses. The students were asked to tell why each had chosen that particular one. Danny, as usual didn't take it very seriously at first. He read John 11:35 "*Jesus wept.*" He said it was chosen because it is the shortest verse in the Bible, which caused Shelly to grimace. Then in a more serious voice he said it was chosen because it showed him how much Jesus loves us all. His sister nodded in approval.

Jerry was the last one to share his Bible verse. He announced it would be Hebrews 12: 1 & 2: "*Therefore, since we are surrounded by so great a cloud of witnesses, let us lay aside every weight, and sin which clings so closely, and let us run with perseverance the race that is set before us, looking to Jesus the pioneer and perfecter of our faith.*" He explained that he had learned in the class how many people had carefully and faithfully made great sacrifices so we could have this church and how many people of the future were holding their breath to see what we will do with it.

Finis: Pages from Patmos

Printed in the United States
By Bookmasters